The Book of Soul

Lamarr Futrell

Published by Lamarr Futrell, 2024.

This is a work of fiction. Similarities to real people, places, or events are entirely coincidental.

THE BOOK OF SOUL

First edition. April 1, 2024.

Copyright © 2024 Lamarr Futrell.

ISBN: 979-8224446452

Written by Lamarr Futrell.

Table of Contents

Chapter I: The Arrival

The purpose of life is to feel like the main character in your own movie. In this life smile through the pain, and don't hold the next person to a higher standard than you can't hold yourself to. Through understanding that I don't know everything, and don't want to know everything. The way that I carry myself came from a gem my granny gave me. Never be so quick to speak when you're emotional, regardless of who's right or wrong in the situation. Understanding life is acknowledging the role that men and women play in society. Adam needed Eve, just as much as Eve needed Adam. Just because you can do it all by yourself, doesn't always mean that you should. But if you're in a position where you don't have a choice but to do something by yourself—just make sure you look like the flyest person doing it. One's purpose does not lie between the lines of settling for the bare minimum. Nor does their life purpose consist of them working in a career that pays well but drains them internally. Sadly, many have failed to live to their fullest potential, as a consequence of allowing distractions, setbacks, mediocrity, or fear to dictate their future. For a period, fear prevented me from sharing my gifts. Fear of my work not being "good enough." Fear of not receiving the recognition I felt I deserved. Fear of my work going astray. Fortunately, I was able to look beyond my fears to trust my intuition. While growing an abundance of self-love, and acknowledgment of my self-worth, I began to grow into who I was meant to become all along. A true renaissance man or woman is so well-versed in his or her culture, and education that they make it their mission to explore the world showcasing their God-given talents through their raw identity. Life isn't about remaining consistent with being a one-shaded individual, but through being consistent in being comfortable in being many shades of yourself without adhering to the constructs you think society is placing on you. Just as I am the epitome of a Renaissance Man, the weight holds the same as it takes a village to raise a child. The first lesson, delegate your funds wisely and respectfully. The key to living a well-balanced lifestyle is by strategically doing what makes sense when it is supposed to make sense—even if it only makes sense to you. As people, we romanticize power and struggle, most times in ways where they should not coincide. The idea of a "perfect world" will always remain as a concept—not because it is impossible, but until we want it to exist. "Happiness is based on a just discrimination of what is necessary, what is neither necessary nor destructive, and what is destructive." The reason there's a disconnect in the proper treatment of the opposite gender is solely due to how men were raised by other men to treat a woman, just as women were taught the same from a woman—instead of leaning on the opposite gender to seek how they truly desire to be treated. I aspire to be a lot like Big Meech by showcasing an experience that celebrates life. Regardless of whether you agree with Big Meech's practices, you must respect what he did for Black people. His influence was what showed us that Black people have what it takes to lead politically, culturally, and economically. We attained resources through mastering the art of finesse, without becoming equipped with the necessary knowledge to be an understanding voice in our own communities by training our people on the true essence of patience and gratitude without being defected by the evils of comparison. Word to the most legendary high school biology teacher: "You don't know what you don't know, if you don't study." When you serve you discover that often the most important things you have to offer are not tangible. With service, what you give out, comes back double in return. Now, upon graduating from Morehouse, my heart lies in righting the wrongs of the "Delmar Divide," in St. Louis, MO. I have aspired to become many things, and each of them consists of me bridging the gap for my people. In church, I was taught that it is better to give than to receive. Through being exposed to life, success to me does not come from what one has done for himself, but how efficient he is in contributing to his people.

Investing in a better industry for tomorrow is going to require investing in the right individuals to do so. Having a powerful voice and using it incorrectly can be more of a detriment than not using it all. This means that instead of relying on Black entertainers to act as activists or politicians—we must support, and invest in the campaigns of those who have the true desire to do so along with the knowledge to properly execute. "I'm not saying I'm gonna rule the world, but I guarantee you that I will spark the brain that will change the world." - Tupac Shakur. As time continues to change, the mindset of one being a voice to the voiceless should transform into one building a voice for the voiceless. In an effort towards becoming an asset through providing people from backgrounds with opportunities of a lifetime. One who has no recollection from which he has come cannot be a service to his or her people. Before stepping into any room your goal should be to make your presence felt through being the life of the party, the flyest in the room, or both—it takes practice to do both because impressions are everything. When it comes to relationships, you must think of people as assets and liabilities. When you have a roster the only way to truly win is by making everybody around you feel like they're the number one draft pick whether they believe it or not because the goal is to make the one beside you feel like they are living in your fantasy with you. When it comes to women, you gotta know the vibes, to know the vibes. If you don't know the vibes, then you just won't know the vibes. Meaning, that you must get to know her, by studying her. Fellas, chivalry is not dead. Consistency is key! Before picking up a woman for a date, get her some flowers. Also, the amount of money you spend/ flash on a date doesn't always equate to the best experience. Instead, plan out a date based on what you perceive her personality to be. The best conversations occur at art museums. The best laughs are held at restaurants. The most fun is had at arcades and outdoor experiences. Culture is defined as the manifestations of human development and intellectual achievement. Examples of culture include music genres, styles, ways of living, and the list goes on. When adapting to a new culture, you expose people to pieces of your culture as well. When exposing people to your culture, or vice versa, people are either going to appreciate your culture or appropriate it. The difference comes through one choosing to pay their respect. Everyone loves a good time, but no one wants to waste time. To get to know her better, allow her to play music from her phone in your car while you're driving—this gives her a sense of control. Remember, the key is to make her feel like she's living in your fantasy with you. Women's problems are not always considered first-hand. For women to have their problems heard, they must work harder, reform has to take place most of the time. Whether a party is on the left, or right does matter. However, some political parties do better in promoting women than others because they realize that equal representation was not enough, but descriptive representation was. Descriptive representation states there must be a similarity between the constituents and representatives. Ida B. Wells was known as a journalist, abolitionist, and feminist. Wells is known mostly for her contributions to women of color. Through her focus on the women's suffrage movement, Wells realized that African American women did not have the education to engage in politics. She grouped Black women from all over to provide them with the proper intellect to do so. Wells' efforts went as far as to grant women the right to vote. W.E.B Du Bois spent his life discovering the notion he deemed as, "the Negro problem". Du Bois was an activist, journalist, historian, and sociologist who spent the span of his life extensively examining race, and the problems that exist amongst races. In theory, Du Bois defines race as a force that divides humans into spiritually distinct groups. Du Bois was also a social reformer who researched the causes of social problems like poverty, suicide, and crime to combat the Negro problem. Before establishing a plan on where to go, one must acknowledge the place from which we've come. Du Bois' focus on his mission towards identifying "the Negro Problem", is why I'm so adamant about solving it in today's time. Having the right women on your team can change your entire trajectory for the best. Keeping the right woman beside you through it all is not easy, but it's simple. Simply, all she wants is someone to feel secure with while having fun—someone with whom she can be serious within escaping the realities of this world. In essence, honesty in the smoothest way is the new way to court someone. Lying is stressful, and finessing can become uncontrollable—just tell her the truth. Women have a vast impact on men. Look at Othello. Look at Adam. Better yet, take a glance back to when Kanye West's mother was present in his life. Beyond that, Infants are brought into the world out of a woman's womb. In education, the top Historically Black College/University is Spelman College, a private liberal arts women's college. Economically, women as breadwinners is becoming more common. Although most of the world has been run with men as overseers. Essentially, women rule the world. Women are gifts, natural givers, and have been exceeding in all facets of life for centuries. In addition to that, "behind every great man, is a great woman." The person who has inspired me to pursue a career in law won a supreme court case with minimal experience. Why? She won a Supreme Court case, without possessing a law degree. Afeni Shakur and twenty other members of the Black Panther Party were charged with conspiracy to kill police officers, and bombing four police stations, five department stores, and the Bronx Botanical Gardens. Shakur's role in the Panther 21 case was vital. Aside from reading several books while in custody, Afeni Shakur had no prior experience in law. However, after bail was posted for thirteen of the twenty-one members (including Shakur) Afeni returned to act as a legal defender for those who were still on trial. In returning, Shakur could prove that the New York City Police Department was corrupt. On May 12, 1971, The Black Panther members that were involved in the case were acquitted of all 156 charges. The Panther 21 case affected the Black community heavily. Who was at the forefront? A black woman. At twenty-one became a section leader of the Harlem Chapter of the Black Panther Party. Afeni Shakur is also the mother of Tupac Shakur. Afeni's impact on Tupac's life is arguably the reason he grew into the person he became as he was more than a rapper, but also an actor, activist, and revolutionist. Tupac's placed more of a heavier impact on modern society than those who have surpassed him in life. Afeni Shakur making it a priority to instill knowledge and wisdom into Tupac is the reason. Dr. Martin Luther King Jr. and Malcolm X complement each other more than they complicate. King and X shared the same goal of pursuing equality for Black people. Malcolm ascribed to the Nation of Islam while King ascribed to the Christian faith. Despite X's focus on their differences, many of their political and religious beliefs overlapped, which impels a commonality between the two. In addition to King's religious views, his political agenda nationalized the global community. Along with X's belief in the Nation of Islam, his political stance lied in Black Nationalism. "Throughout our history in this country, radical black political leadership has emerged from religious settings, whether they be Christian, Islam, or less recognized spiritual paths" (Hooks). Their religious beliefs coincide with their political views because much of their political agendas inspired their religious doctrines. The idea of a global community calls for unity amongst all people, or nations. In influencing unity, the focal point of King's political agenda was love. "Much of King's focus on love as the fundamental principle that should guide the freedom struggle was directed toward upholding his belief in nonviolence" (Hooks). King does not see love as sentimental instead, he sees love as a strong force that will unite all nations of people. Primarily, King focused on loving the enemy: "While we abhor segregation, we shall love the segregationist. This is the only way to create the beloved community" (King), The primary goal of the Civil Rights Movement was to influence white people to view black people as actual humans. King used the biblical principle: "Thou shalt love thy neighbor as thyself" (Matthew 22:39) as he felt that was the only way for Black people to attain equality. The ideology that coincides with love, is justice. In terms of justice, Black nationalism is a political ideal that seeks to advance the development of Black people. Malcolm X conformed to Black nationalism as he opposed the idea of Black Americans integrating with White Americans. "He rejected the idea that blacks in America were a minority. Rather he contended that they were a part of the colored majority in the world," (Sengstacke) In X's stance of reclamation for black pride, he was extremely zealous in advocating for Black independence. In his advocacy, Malcolm X was one of many leaders who did not believe in loving the enemy, in hopes that the leader will return the compassion. In terms of religion, X's messages pertained to God's relationship with society and one's fight for justice in it. "When Malcolm X identified the fight for justice as the central religious act, his messages were usually misunderstood." I believe the misunderstandings came from people's awareness of what God can do, instead of what He can do for all. Also, many of X's messages were unorthodox as he seemed to promote hate and violence. Moreover, X was obedient to the Black Muslim Religion. Both men had different perspectives on the movement. However, many of the ways they went about attaining justice were similar. Both men were men of God. Dr. Martin Luther King Jr. was a Baptist minister. Both men were educated. While King pursued the route of formal education, X chose to be self-taught. Malcolm X and Dr. Martin Luther King Jr were prominent figures. However, their influence did not come from them alone as their influencers were Asian. Mahatma Gandhi played an integral role in King's nonviolent movement. Yuri Kochiyama played an essential role in influencing X's Black nationalist movement. During King's visit to India, he found a variety of ways to implicate Gandhi's principles back into his movements. King recollects being looked upon as a brother "with the color of their skin being something of an asset". Years later, in his 'I Have A Dream speech, King charged citizens of America from all backgrounds with a similar notion. "I have a dream that my four little children will one day live in a nation where they will not be judged by the color of their skin, but by the content of their character." Essentially, Dr. King wanted unity amongst all races of people, by using love as the focal point of his political agenda. Although Malcolm X globalized Black nationalism, X impacted the Asian community as well. Foremost. X was vocal in ensuring that people of color were aware of their identities, and heritage. In The Impact of Malcolm X Asian-American Politics and Activism, Kochiyama recalls X asking, "If you don't know who you are and where you come from, how can you know which direction to go?" Asian Americans perceived X as the symbol for being fearless against oppression, in contesting racism. X and Kochiyama share similarities in being people of color fighting for justice. Yuri was raised on a similar belief as Malcolm. A belief that one should become aware of their heritage, and ancestry for them to be able to take pride in their identity. In time, many tend to find all reasons why King and X contrast, even as they are parallel to each other. King and X were both advocates for Black power, freedom, and equality. No, they were not ascribed to the same religion. No, they did not have the same approach in their fight for justice. Although King followed the global community's agenda, and X Black nationalism; love and justice were the face of their political stances. However, they stood at the forefront of the movement, in agreement for the development of Black people. Also, their influences affected people in all nations. All leaders must have integrity, respect, and humility. In an effort towards becoming an asset through providing people from backgrounds with opportunities of a lifetime. Stacey Abrams felt that one's ambitions should not be limited to a title or position. Hence, one should focus on the "why," rather than the "what". Malcolm X and Dr. King were both ahead of their time. Regarding one's ethnicity and socioeconomic status, King and X were advocating for the same issues we are still fighting to abolish in modern times. In fact, how they took initiative left us as people, spoiled. As struggling people, we are not taking initiative in the way we should. When an initiative is taken, it is limited to protests when more can be done. Protesting during the Civil Rights Era was powerful because it was the most that could be done. With access to greater technology, voting rights, and capital we have the potential to shift the negatives; under one condition, we must unite as one. Cultural adaptation is the process one goes through when adapting to a new culture. The axiom can be both beneficial and a detriment to the people. As one is adapting to a new culture, he, or she is also introducing pieces of their culture. With that, cultural adaptation relates to conflict theory which views social and economic units as resources of struggle amongst groups or classes. In detail, conflict theory is used to maintain the dominance of those in power. Cultural adaptation relates to the conflict theory because it also makes room for one to experience cultural appreciation versus cultural appropriation. King was a detail-oriented man with a plan. However, when people acknowledge King's efforts, many often neglect to respect the influences that developed him into creating the legacy that he left. "Communism is a judgment against our failure to make democracy real." Specifically, King's initiative would yield toward uniting all people, and not being limited to only protesting but attaining more power. "Every man of humane convictions must decide on the protest that best suits his convictions, but we must all protest." Due to the social constructs that stem out of oppression, (or interlocking oppression) we must fight for all, united, and with a plan. Furthermore, Dr. King was indeed ahead of his time. How he took initiative left us spoiled, and limited. With greater access to technology and capital, we have the potential to shift the negatives to positive—under one condition, we must unite as one. As I navigate this urban jungle, I've come to realize that life is like starring in your own movie. You gotta smile through the pain and never hold someone to a higher standard than you hold yourself. My granny dropped some wisdom on me that I've carried like a precious gem: never let your emotions speak before you do. It's a lesson I've learned the hard way, but it's made me who I am today. Understanding life means understanding the roles men and women play in society. We need each other, plain and simple. And while it's great to be independent, sometimes you gotta embrace the help around you, and if you're in a solo mission, you better make sure you're doing it in style. Life's not about settling for less or just chasing a paycheck. It's about living up to your fullest potential, even if it means facing your fears head-on. I used to let fear hold me back, but I've learned to trust my instincts and embrace who I am. I'm on a mission to be a modern Renaissance person, showcasing my talents and culture wherever I go. Life's not about fitting into a box society puts you in; it's about being comfortable in your own skin, in all its shades. When it comes to relationships, you gotta treat people like assets, not liabilities. Make them feel like they're the MVP of your team, whether it's the life of the party or your ride-or-die. And let's talk about women. They're the backbone of society, the real rulers of the world. Just look at the history books—women have been making moves since day one. From Afeni Shakur to Stacey Abrams, they're the true changemakers. Speaking of history, Dr. King and Malcolm X may have had different approaches, but they shared the same goal: equality. They stood as beacons of hope, showing us that change is possible, even when the odds are stacked against you. But it's not just about looking back; it's about moving forward. We've got the tools and the technology to make real change, but only if we come together as one. We can't let fear or division hold us back. We've gotta take the initiative and fight for what's right. So here I am, sharing my art with the world, one Instagram post at a time. It might seem small, but every like, every share, it's all part of the bigger picture. We've all got a role to play in this movie called life, and I'm ready to make mine count.

Chapter II: Too Deep For The Intro

In a world filled with visions and aspirations, Lenny Speaks, a young dreamer with a spirit fueled by the legends of the past, embarked on an epic journey. It all began with a vision, a vision that transported me to the realms of the past, where icons like Marvin Gaye, Dr. King, Beyonce, Bernie Mac, Tupac, and Suge Knight awaited, their words echoing in my mind as I sought a higher purpose, a divine path. My prayer was simple: that each of these luminaries, past and present, would step into their destinies, unburdened by the shackles of yesterday's troubles. As I poured my heart into this quest to find God and myself, I found myself in a season of divine isolation. Yet, little did I know that God had been trailing me all along, like a silent guardian in the shadows. And so, with Marvin as my companion, we embarked on our quest to uncover the truth of what was going on. Dr. King, on the other hand, pleaded with the world to see beyond the surface, to recognize character over color. From a young boy who couldn't foresee the trials and tribulations ahead to a Morehouse College graduate. When I was born again, I had discovered my true name – Lenny Speaks. The birth of Lenny Speaks traced back to nights cruising through South Saint Louis in my Great-Grandfather's Cadillac Deville with The Thrill Is Gone playing through the cassette tape. The thrill of those journeys inspired a hunger for knowledge and wisdom. I had dreamt of becoming a mogul until I realized I already was one. Legacy, I mused, was tied to one's beliefs and principles. As the narrative continued, I navigated through the intricate realms of truth and language. Truth was the lighthouse guiding my path, but language was my vessel. It allowed me to express thoughts, seek understanding, and question the validity of statements. Two philosophers, Ramsey and Strawson, had their say on truth, but I sought a deeper understanding, a truth beyond language. I believed in a truth that transcended words, one rooted in beliefs, the unknown, and the future. But my journey wasn't just about philosophy. It was a call to action, a call to change the narrative of Black music. It was a call to recognize the power of technology and culture in the music business. The three record giants – Warner, Universal, and Sony – held the keys, but technology was shifting the landscape. I knew the importance of relationships, mentors, and negotiation. I urged others not to let differences in beliefs deter them from seizing opportunities. I understood that building establishments required strategy, perseverance, and a long-term vision. As I reflected on my experiences, I highlighted the significance of relationships. I learned from legends in The Recording Academy, men who imparted wisdom and the importance of positive energy. I understood that knowledge was power, and it was crucial to share and uplift others. The narrative shifted towards the realm of love and relationships. I shared insights into courtship, emphasizing the importance of chivalry and consistency. I encouraged men to understand and appreciate women, treating them as assets, not liabilities. I recognized that women held immense power, shaping men's lives and the world itself. From music to politics, women's influence was undeniable. My quest for truth, education, culture, and love became an epic tale of self-discovery and transformation. In a world where one man's vision could ignite change, Lenny Speaks had become a force to be reckoned with, a Renaissance Man on a mission to rewrite the narrative and build bridges between hearts and minds. Lenny Speaks was a man of many talents and interests. He was a philosopher, a creator, and a thinker who questioned the world around him. His thoughts were like ripples in a pond, spreading outwards in all directions, touching the hearts and minds of those fortunate enough to listen. "Can I vent real quick?", a question he often asked himself as if he was asking the world. The question wasn't for anyone in particular, but for his own musings, his own internal dialogues that ran deeper than most people could fathom. "See the woman, I need a woman who can teach me how to dress through the way she dresses," he mused, his eyes gazing at the world through a lens of longing. "To teach me how to love through her imperfections. A woman who can submit for the same reason I would want to submit to her. Not for any reason though." His voice carried the weight of his desires, desires that transcended the superficial and ventured into the realm of the profound. "One of the hardest things men fail to understand is the best thing you can find in a woman is her strength to submit to you while also acknowledging her worth as well." Lenny's words were like a revelation, a truth that had eluded many. He understood that strength and vulnerability could coexist, that love could be a dance of equals. Lenny's thoughts then meandered to deeper societal issues, issues that tugged at his heart and compelled him to speak his truth. "The difficulty is that the 'educated negro' is compelled to live and move among his people whom he has been taught to despise." He knew that unity was a powerful force, yet it was often hindered by the divisions that society had sown. "Of all the various ethnicities that exist, African Americans are the only group of individuals who find it hard to unite and grow together as one." Lenny's voice was tinged with sadness, for he saw the potential squandered, the lost. "Why are we such a detriment to each other? When we move out of our communities to better ourselves, why is it such a task at hand for us to come back as one?" As he quoted Carter G. Woodson, "the negro thus educated is a hopeless liability of the race," Lenny's heart ached. He knew that education should empower, not divide. He wanted to change the narrative, to bridge the gaps that separated his people. Lenny's heart was always with his community, and he believed in the power of unity and support. "Attending a Historically Black College or University, regardless of the institution, is a start." He knew that investment in Black communities and institutions was vital, for it was they who had built the nation. As his thoughts turned to movements like Black Lives Matter, Lenny saw the potential for change. "Black Lives Matter was founded to demand changes in economic development, police brutality, education, and conscious awareness for the Black Community." He understood the importance of providing a platform for people to speak their truth, to stand against injustice, and to honor the legacy of those who came before. Lenny's words left a lasting impression, a call to action and a call for unity. "Modern society is in constant search for the next Malcolm, Martin, Rosa, or Harriet to be the voice for this generation when we already exist." Before enrolling at Morehouse College, my dream was to return to my hometown as a hero, but destiny had a different plan for me. During my time at Morehouse, I embraced a new identity - Lenny Speaks. The path to success varies for each of us, but the starting point is often similar, and the ultimate goal is the same. While our origins may differ, we all aspire to create a heaven on Earth, at least I certainly do. I've been a student of the game ever since I first stepped into my Kindergarten classroom at Hodgen Elementary. However, I made a significant mistake by devoting too much time to English and not enough to Mathematics. It was a lesson I didn't fully grasp until I arrived at Morehouse College, where I lost myself in the pursuit of proving my humanity to others. Fortunately, I had the guidance of a true OG in my life, my Great-Grandfather Clyde Davis Sr. He used to take me on rides in his pristine '99 Cadillac Deville, complete with maroon seats and colored tints from a bygone era. It was a clean ride, just missing some gold BBS wheels. Beyond his style, I adopted his posture, walk, and speech. He taught me the genuine art of greeting others with love, saying, "What's good, big dawg!" He also introduced me to the world of investing, a realm where our family's blessings were guided by foresight and vision. When I arrived at college, I had already mastered the social game. I learned the importance of connecting with people, whether you know them or not, as you never know who they might become, but they'll always remember your face. Having fun is great, but it's crucial to keep your priorities straight – the bag always comes first. However, what defines the "bag" varies from person to person. To me, it means creating a life filled with freedom, wealth, love, peace, and happiness. Let's address something - fake friendships are weird. No need to explain further, but it had to be said. Create a three-month plan and execute it with the same dedication as if you were working on a year-long project, even if time is limited. I look up to Big Meech, but I also aspire to tell stories like Quincy Jones. Quincy's work is a testament to adding a personal touch to everything you create, ensuring that it's recognized and respected. Although I wasn't born during Quincy's prime, his work has been a constant presence in my life without me even realizing it. Emotions should never cloud judgment, as it can be perilous. Supporting someone means offering emotional, instrumental, informational, or appraisal assistance. Social Support Theory emphasizes the importance of providing aid to prevent individuals from resorting to a survivor's mindset, which can lead to reckless behavior. Social support is also a coping resource, and it plays a pivotal role in our lives. Morehouse College provides the resources needed for students to put in their ten thousand hours while instilling character and leadership skills. The transformation from a Man of Morehouse to a Morehouse Man is a special journey. The Brown Street Connection is unique, where you can casually encounter Shaquille O'Neal or Samuel L. Jackson while strolling past King Chapel. The sauce you gain from attending Morehouse College, Spelman College, or Clark Atlanta University is unparalleled. My high school journey involved finessing my way through, learning valuable lessons before I set foot in Morehouse, praying for a chance. However, my desire to become a hometown hero nearly blinded me to the unique journey ahead. Atlanta has a knack for making everyone feel important, especially when you know people, and it seemed like I knew everybody. As I put in my ten thousand hours, I learned that studying wisely is the key. Embrace the journey, as each experience teaches something unique, regardless of whether you filled the space with your presence as you wished or not. I've curated various playlists that tell my story and represent different aspects of my personality, interests, and experiences.

They range from nostalgia to self-improvement and from relaxation to exploration of different shades of Black culture. Each playlist holds a piece of my identity. Through connecting with individuals, I've gained a deeper understanding of the qualities that define leaders. As time passed, I began to feel that I was not where I needed to be, both internally and externally. Success, I realized, comes from self-awareness and understanding the environment in which you operate. Reflecting on my first semester of college, I understood that success came from knowing expectations and procedures, focusing, doing excellent work, treating classes seriously, and seeking help when needed. I was an adult now, with friends and family investing in my success. It was my duty to make the most of my current situation. I've experienced ups and downs, and it took losing my Great-Grandmother to understand the true essence of my vision. Lenny Speaks began to emerge during my Junior year of high school when I became involved in extracurricular activities as I began labeling myself as the goat. My Senior year was a whirlwind of experiences as I prepared for college. Graduation marked a significant milestone, but I wish I had known then what I know now as I prepared for my first semester at Morehouse College. Lenny pulled up to his first math class at Morehouse wearing a suit on a sweltering Atlanta day, trying to keep up with his Morehouse brothers. The atmosphere at a school graced by legends like Samuel L. Jackson, Dr. Martin Luther King Jr., Steve Pamon, Spike Lee, and many others were electrifying. Yet, the immense pressure I placed on myself hindered me from fully enjoying my college experience. Ironically, when I arrived at Morehouse I, as Lamarr realized my Great-Grandfather had placed such a task of me taking care of the women of the family as he was on his deathbed. In my collegiate moment, it felt as if he was righting his wrongs through raising me to be upright in his time with me. Suddenly, it even made sense as to why he would often find peace through sitting at the kitchen table throughout the day, and my Great-Grandmother enjoyed sitting in the living room. "To be absent from the body is to be present in the spirit." These words echoed in my mind as I stood by the grave of my beloved Great-Grandmother, Rebecca Davis. Losing her was a profound loss, but her memory continued to guide me every step of the way. It felt like she was still with me, her prayers surrounding me like a protective cloak. I found solace in the gospel song "Order My Steps." When I listened to it, I could hear her voice singing along, and it brought tears to my eyes. She had left a spiritual imprint on my soul, a legacy of faith and love that I carried in my heart. In the wake of her passing, I chose to accept the calling that God had placed upon my life—to help people heal. I understood that healing went beyond the physical; it encompassed the spiritual and mental realms as well. To truly win in this life, I needed to be kept spiritually, mentally, and physically, and I knew I couldn't do it alone. Before embarking on any new journey, I made it a habit to seek God's guidance and ask Him to set the atmosphere every step of the way. It was a practice that had served me well, a reminder that I was not alone in this grand adventure called life. I could almost hear my Great-Grandmother's voice encouraging me to continue. "But you see, Granny, knowing what to know is just as important as knowing who to know. People are very sensitive to their time, which is why my intent in maintaining relationships has always been to add value to those around me. If you have it in you, teach them to do the same." A smile played on my lips as I remembered Henny's words to me. "Henny saw something in me that I only thought I saw in myself," I shared. "He said, 'You're the glue that brings everything and everybody together.' It was a powerful reminder of the impact we can have on others. Granny had always taught me the importance of balance in life, and I continued in that vein. "The key to living a well-balanced lifestyle is by strategically doing what makes sense when it's supposed to make sense—even if it only makes sense to you." I delved into a topic that had been on my mind lately. "As people, we tend to romanticize power and struggle, often in ways where they shouldn't coincide. The idea of a 'perfect world' will always remain a concept, not because it's impossible, but until we want it to exist." My voice took on a more serious tone as I addressed an issue that weighed heavily on my heart. "As people, we've assigned titles and roles to everything and everyone, often down to gender roles. We talk about appointing women as world leaders, but sometimes we don't truly believe in it when it comes to giving them the platforms they rightfully deserve." I sighed, thinking about the disconnect in how we treat each other. "The reason there's a disconnect in the proper treatment of the opposite gender is solely due to how men were raised by other men to treat a woman, just as women were taught the same from a woman. Instead of leaning on the opposite gender to seek how they truly desire to be treated, we need to have open and honest conversations." Through being exposed to life, success to me does not come from what one has done for himself, but how efficient he is in contributing to his people." As I finished my story, I felt Granny's presence, her spirit embracing me in a comforting embrace. It was a conversation that spanned generations, and I knew that her legacy of love and wisdom would continue to guide me on my journey. Lenny sat in King Chapel, surrounded by the hushed ambiance of the historic space. The chapel had always been a place of solace for him, a haven where he could think and reflect. Today, he was working with CASA, a commitment he took seriously. But as he worked, his mind wandered to deeper aspirations. "Often we as humans read and write more than we talk," Lenny mused, his fingers tapping lightly on the table. "For example, after waking up from either a nap or from the night before, after yawning and stretching, you use your phone as a clock to read what time it is and any missed notifications." He adjusted his posture, leaning forward as he delved into his thoughts. "As a student, I understand that it was the gained experience I have in reading and writing that's gotten me where I am now, and it's going to take me where I need to go. Writing expresses who you are as a person, whereas reading helps you understand others." Lenny's eyes sparkled with the passion he felt for the written word. "The mind is a muscle. Think of reading and writing as doing crunches and pushups. Crunches help your core to grow stronger, and push-ups help your arms to grow stronger. Writing helps one part of your brain to get stronger, and reading helps the other." He paused, memories of his early days as a writer flooding back. "I started writing stories and movie scripts at the early age of nine years old. As I developed, I even became successful in poetry and spoken word. My ultimate task, not only as a creative person but as a person in general, is to do or say what hasn't been done before." Lenny's voice grew more contemplative as he continued. "I've also gained a lot of discipline since I've been writing. I believe there's always at least one option left, even when it isn't any at all. No is not an option. For me to feel like I've completed a piece, I have to know and feel like it's better than the last, as a sign of growth." He leaned back in his chair, gazing up at the high ceiling of the chapel. "Take a moment, and ask yourself, 'how did I get to where I am today?' Your answer is in the first paragraph, third sentence, fifteenth, and seventeenth word." Lenny's thoughts turned to the power of reading. "Although I don't like reading as much, it is highly useful. Reading takes you to a world of imagination, showing you nothing is impossible in this world. By reading, you are visualizing something from a different perspective or angle to see a thing you've known, but in many ways, almost like watching a movie several times and always expecting a different ending." His mind then drifted to his ultimate goal. "My only goal is to master myself. Why search for gold if my soul is what I possess? In other words, why seek gold if my soul holds more wealth? I never knew the complexion of my skin could hold so much power. I knew actions spoke louder than words, but by me being a young black man, I didn't know they'd be even louder." Lenny's words hung in the air, a testament to his determination and the path he was forging for himself. He knew the journey ahead would be filled with challenges, but he was ready to face them head-on. As he sat in King Chapel, he felt the weight of his aspirations and the desire to make a lasting impact on the world. In the bustling heart of Atlanta, Lenny Speaks, a student at Morehouse College, was juggling his demanding coursework, part-time jobs, and extracurricular activities. Lenny's resume told a story of ambition and perseverance, a testament to his desire to leave an indelible mark on the world. Lenny's journey started with his role as an independent contractor for Amazon Flex in his hometown of St. Louis, Missouri. He meticulously handled packages weighing up to 60 pounds, showing a knack for organization and an unwavering commitment to his responsibilities. He took pride in performing regular safety inspections on his delivery truck, ensuring that it was always in optimal condition. His meticulous nature even led him to inspect each product for defects before accepting them, thereby saving the company valuable time and resources. His move to Atlanta marked the beginning of his rise in the world of sales. Joining Paces Worldwide as a Sales Specialist in August 2022, he was tasked with developing and maintaining client relationships. Lenny excelled in providing consultative enterprise solutions, planning and presenting solution-based sales and marketing presentations. He wasn't merely a salesperson; he was a problem solver. His journey took a more creative turn as he joined the JBL Campus HBCU SoundSessions Program under HARMAN International in April 2021. As a mentee in this prestigious program, Lenny rubbed shoulders with industry executives in the music and consumer electronics sector. His drive to learn from the best and the brightest was evident. As a Brand Ambassador for Beats x Books, Lenny established himself as a valuable connector. He built and leveraged a network of influential local partners, covering a wide range of cultural and creative backgrounds. He co-hosted sessions focusing on artist development, brand awareness, and financial literacy, and his keen eye for marketing material increased sales and expanded the client base. Think It's a Game Records benefited from Lenny's creative insight as he worked as a Creative Intern. He contributed to event preparation, managed event recaps, and established an in-house knowledge base for marketing content. Lenny was always thinking a step ahead, his contributions instrumental to the company's growth. Lenny's role as a Creative Director at Kylar.IO in St. Louis showcased his strategic thinking. He used audience research and data insights to strengthen creative work. His creative leadership and brand expertise were valuable assets to the Kylar.IO platform, and he spearheaded the creative and production division of the Kylar.IO Blockchain Conference in 2019. His brand ambassadorship at BET in Atlanta was a testament to his consumer-centric approach. Lenny had a unique ability to examine marketing material from a consumer's perspective, ensuring the delivery of great customer experiences. His work on a team with others contributed to generating over 700 new users for BET's online streaming service. Lenny's commitment to his community was evident through his role as a Teacher Assistant at McCluer North High School. He welcomed and assisted students and provided support during teacher absences. His involvement in creating educational plans and activities helped students understand the curriculum better. But Lenny's journey wasn't limited to the professional world. He was actively engaged in numerous extracurricular activities at Morehouse College, where he was passionate about leadership development, community service, and networking. As a part of the Emerging Student Leaders, Morehouse Business Association, Morehouse Marketing Association, Morehouse Pre-Alumni Association, OHUBxSXSW, DECA, Principal's Advisory Council, Future Business Leaders of America, and Men On Business, Lenny displayed his dedication to personal growth and community impact. Lenny's desire to excel extended beyond academics and career pursuits. He actively participated in events such as YouTube Black FanFest, Music Production & Recording Sciences Workshops, and the Revolt Summit: The Atlanta Edition. These experiences further enriched his diverse skill set. As Lenny looked at his resume, it was more than just a list of jobs and activities; it was a roadmap of his journey. Each role, each experience, and each endeavor had contributed to his growth. He aspired to be a creative director, a business developer, a marketer, and a sales expert. With his determination, resilience, and commitment to excellence, Lenny Speaks was undoubtedly on the path to becoming one of the greatest in his chosen field. Lenny's journey from the heart of St. Louis to the hallowed halls of Morehouse College was more than a geographic transition; it was a transformation of the soul. His story, filled with dreams, heartache, and unwavering determination, would touch the hearts of many. In the heart of St. Louis, where the streets hummed with life and stories of survival echoed through the alleys, Lenny was a young man with a vision. He saw beyond the challenges that surrounded him, the obstacles that had become part of his daily life. Instead of succumbing to the harsh realities of his neighborhood, he chose to dream. "Instead of fiending, I'm dreaming. Instead of doubting, I'm believing," Lenny often told himself. He had a fire within him, a belief that a change was on the horizon, just waiting to manifest itself. Lenny's inspiration came from the music of legends like Sam Cooke, whose voice carried the hopes and dreams of a generation. One fateful day, August 19, 2009, Lenny's life took an unexpected turn. It began like any other day, with a routine trip to the dentist for a teeth cleaning. Lenny was feeling good, hopeful, and full of life. Little did he know that this day would bring news that would test his strength and resilience. As he left the dentist's office, a sense of dread hung in the air. Lenny overheard his grandmother's voice, quivering with emotion, as she spoke urgently on the phone. "Big Daddy," his great-grandfather and a beloved figure in their family, had been rushed to the hospital. Lenny's heart sank, and a feeling of helplessness washed over him. He wished he could be by his great-grandfather's side, to offer comfort and share his thoughts and feelings. But life had other plans. Lenny had been dropped off at school that day, and the physical distance prevented him from being there during this crucial moment. He clung to the last words he heard his great-grandfather say, "Jefferson," a name that held a deeper meaning yet to be uncovered. It was during this time of uncertainty and grief that Lenny's mind connected the dots, like a lightning bolt of revelation. He remembered the stories his great-grandfather had shared, stories of their family's heritage. One name that stood out was Thomas Edison, the famed inventor. He realized that within the tales and lessons passed down through generations, there were messages waiting to be deciphered, meant for those who carried the family legacy forward. In the years that followed, Lenny grew and matured, his dreams evolving and expanding. He felt like he was in the lead now, steering through life's obstacles with a sense of purpose and determination. He believed in making the impossible possible, in turning dreams into reality. With each step, Lenny carried the memory of his great-grandfather, the lessons learned, and the love shared. He thought of the mixtape he might create one day, a rhythm of hope and inspiration for others to vibe to. He even toyed with the idea of writing a novel, one that would touch hearts and inspire change, perhaps even becoming a bestseller on a shelf somewhere. Lenny's journey was far from over, but he wore his Nike sneakers not just for himself but for the people around him. He knew that his dreams were bigger than himself, and he was ready to chase them, not for his own health, but for the well-being and upliftment of those he loved and the community he called home.Lenny Speaks, formerly known as Lamarr Terell Futrell, is a name that has grown to represent hope and change in his beloved hometown of St. Louis. His journey from South Saint Louis to Morehouse College was nothing short of transformative, and it's a story that resonates with everyone who hears it. Lenny's roots trace back to St. Louis, a city marred by the infamous Delmar Divide, often described as "legal segregation." It's a division that cuts through communities, creating disparities in opportunities and resources.

Lenny, however, sees this divide as a challenge to be conquered, not an obstacle to be feared. From a young age, Lenny had a deep spiritual foundation instilled in him. His upbringing in the church taught him that everyone has a calling, a purpose in life. He firmly believes that he was put on this Earth to create experiences, open doors of opportunity, and help others find their true selves. During his collegiate journey at Morehouse College, Lenny embarked on a mission to create an innovative art space. This space isn't just about art; it's a place where individuals can pursue careers they're passionate about while gaining the financial literacy needed to make a successful living. Lenny recognizes that in America, communities like his contribute significantly to labor and economics, yet they suffer disproportionately from poverty and a lack of resources. His initiative aims to change that narrative. Lenny often speaks about the concept of "social imagination," a term that describes the ability to connect personal troubles to larger societal issues. He sees problems like gentrification, resource disparities, and the denial of opportunities based on one's identity as grave injustices. He doesn't just see these issues; he confronts them head-on, striving to make a difference. In a world that often romanticizes power and struggle, Lenny envisions a "perfect world" where happiness is based on what is necessary, not destructive. He questions the gender roles that persist in society and believes that women, with their unique ability to bring life into the world, are more than capable of running it. Lenny Speaks is not just a name; it's a movement. It's a testament to the power of one individual's belief in themselves and their commitment to making a positive change in their community. Through his journey, he inspires others to believe in their calling, question the status quo, and work tirelessly to create a more equitable world for all.

Chapter III: The Story of Lenny Speaks

It was said that this elusive budtender had the dankest bud in town and was known for his eccentricity. After a series of hushed conversations and cryptic directions, the journey took him deep into the heart of an deserted yet distant route, far away from the city's prying eyes. "One way in, one way out", I recall him saying. The path grew increasingly eerie as he ventured further into the unknown, the headlights of his car casting long, ghostly shadows. He had long, unruly hair, wore round sunglasses indoors, and was surrounded by a haze of smoke. " Lenny had always been adventurous, and his quest for excitement. often led him into situations most people wouldn't dare to explore. But nothing could have prepared him for the shocking encounter he was about to experience. One gloomy evening, Lenny received a message from a friend hinting at an opportunity to score some high-quality weed. The message was cryptic, only providing an address and a vague promise of a new plug who had the best product in town. Intrigued and fueled by his thirst for adventure, Lenny decided to check it out. The address took him to a desolate, industrial area on the outskirts of the city. The rain began to pour, adding an extra layer of gloom to the eerie atmosphere. Lenny's GPS led him down a long, winding path that seemed to go on forever, with no end in sight. The road was flanked by dark, foreboding trees that reached out like skeletal hands, making him feel like he was entering a nightmare. Finally, Lenny arrived at an old house. windows and walls gave it an ominous aura. Lenny parked his car and took a deep breath, hesitating for a moment before entering his home. Inside, the house was dimly lit, with the pungent smell of marijuana wafting through the air. Lenny cautiously approached a group of men who were huddled in the corner, their faces obscured by shadows. "I'm here for the hookup," Lenny whispered nervously, trying to hide his anxiety. One of the men emerged from the darkness, and Lenny couldn't believe his eyes. He was a young man, dressed in all black and sporting a grin. His cold, piercing blue eyes were the stuff of you only see in dreams and movies. "You're looking for the good stuff, huh?" the man said in a low, gravelly voice. Lenny nodded, swallowing hard. He was taken aback by the sight of this young dealer who seemed straight out of a crime movie. The young man handed Lenny a bag filled with the greenest, stickiest buds he had ever seen. Lenny could hardly contain his excitement as he felt the weight of the bag in his hand. Lenny had always believed that knowledge was a torch that should be passed down to the next generation. He saw himself not only as a student of life but also as a teacher, especially when it came to mentoring young minds. His mentees were like sponges, eager to soak up the wisdom he had to offer. "Culture," Lenny began, "is a reflection of who we are, where we come from, and what we value. When you enter a new culture, remember to respect it. Share your own culture, but do it with humility and the intention of fostering understanding." His mentees nodded, taking notes and digesting his words. They knew that Lenny had a way of making complex ideas seem simple and relatable. Lenny's voice took on a softer tone as he continued, "When it comes to relationships, remember that it's not about control but about connection. Give others a sense of agency, let them share their passions, and create a shared experience. That's where true connection happens." He paused, allowing his mentees to reflect on the importance of building meaningful relationships. Switching gears, Lenny delved into a topic close to his heart: women's issues and representation. "Women's problems often go unheard, and it's our duty to change that," he said. "Look at the trailblazers like Ida B. Wells and W.E.B. Du Bois. They worked tirelessly to empower marginalized communities, especially women. We should follow in their footsteps and strive for equal and descriptive representation." Lenny's mentees were inspired by the stories of these historical figures, realizing the importance of advocating for women's rights and empowerment in today's world. As the evening went on, Lenny's mentees soaked up his wisdom like sponges, cherishing every moment of their mentorship session. They knew that having Lenny in their corner was a gift, and they left the coffee shop that night with a deeper understanding of the world and their role in it. For Lenny, pouring wisdom into his mentees was not just a responsibility; it was a calling. He believed that by shaping the minds of the next generation, he could contribute to a brighter and more enlightened future for all. Lenny leaned back, his mentees absorbing the depth of his words about cultural adaptation and its ties to conflict theory. He continued, "Cultural adaptation isn't just about fitting into a new culture; it's also about maintaining our own identity while appreciating others. It's a delicate balance, much like the power dynamics seen in conflict theory. Those in power often maintain dominance, but it's our responsibility to ensure it doesn't lead to cultural appropriation." As he shifted to the story of Prince, Lenny's mentees listened intently. "Ownership is everything, my friends," he said with conviction. "Prince understood this, and he fought for control over his music. He faced challenges, but he never let his emotions interfere with business. It's a lesson in standing up for what's rightfully yours." Lenny delved into leadership philosophies, his voice unwavering. "Leadership is about more than just power; it's about purpose. Your purpose, your unique identity, sets you apart. It's what drives you to make a difference, whether you're a situational leader, a transactional leader, or a transformational leader." He touched on the importance of moral reasoning. "Our emotions can be powerful, but we must use good reasoning and impartiality in our moral judgments. Emotions should guide us, not cloud our judgment." Lenny talked about support and its various forms. "Support is essential, whether it's emotional, instrumental, informational, or appraisal. We all need it, and we should be there for each other. Building strong relationships and connections is how we thrive." Finally, he circled back to the power of religion and politics. "Religion and politics have been intertwined in our history, influencing our Constitution and our values. But we must remember the importance of freedom and tolerance in a diverse society. It's about finding harmony between shared identity and goodwill." Lenny concluded his session with a smile, leaving his mentees with a wealth of knowledge to ponder. His words weren't just about understanding the world; they were a call to action, a reminder that each of them had the power to shape their lives and society for the better. Lenny's mentees listened intently as he delved into the intricacies of language, truth, and semantics. His words resonated with them, making them question the very essence of communication and understanding in their modern society. He began with the notion of living in a society where every detail of one's life can be shared and exposed, thanks to technology and social media. "We must question our direction and the parallels between us and the society we live in," Lenny emphasized. He urged them to reflect on the impact of technology on their lives and the world around them. As he transitioned to discussing Babylonian heroes, Lenny challenged their understanding of heroism. "A true hero," he explained, "is not just someone with power, but someone who learns humility, compassion, and the ability to turn wrongs into rights. Gilgamesh's transformation from arrogance to compassion is a lesson in true heroism." Lenny continued by exploring the concept of truth. He quoted various philosophers, emphasizing the importance of language in understanding truth. "Language is the vehicle of thought," he said. "To be understood, one must not only grasp the meaning of words but also know how to use them effectively." He concluded with the idea that language requires consciousness and attentiveness. "We must be present in our understanding of language and semantics, as it is the key to effective communication and understanding," he stressed. Lenny's mentees left the session with their minds buzzing with thoughts about language, truth, heroism, and the impact of technology on society. His words had sparked a profound contemplation that would stay with them long after their meeting ended. Though Lenny was from Saint

Louis, Atlanta was similar to his second home. The streets were filled with teachers, preachers, players, gangsters and school buses." Lenny sat in his English Composition Course at Morehouse College, his mind buzzing with thoughts about the power of the human mind and the responsibilities that came with it. As he listened to his professor lecture about the importance of effective communication, he couldn't help but reflect on the words he had written in his essay. "People place themselves where they want to be," he had written, thinking about how individuals often choose their paths in life based on their aspirations. Lenny believed that people were shaped and guided by those they admired, whether in a physical or figurative sense. It was a fundamental truth he had come to understand as he grew older. His thoughts then turned to a darker aspect of human nature. "If a man loses his mind, he will lose everything," he had stated in his essay. Lenny knew that the mind was a fragile thing, and once it was compromised, a person's entire world could crumble. He pondered the dangerous notion that someone with the power to control another's thoughts could essentially command them, leading to a loss of individuality and autonomy. He couldn't help but draw parallels to the struggles of historical figures like Malcolm X and Martin Luther King Jr. Malcolm X had been acutely aware of the power of the mind, consistently asserting that Black people had been brainwashed. On the other hand, King had embodied the principle of "mind over matter" by advocating for nonviolence in the face of injustice. Lenny admired their approaches, each rooted in a deep understanding of the human psyche. His mind then shifted to the importance of mental health. "As people, we must learn to prioritize our mental health by healing, seeking peace, and seeking out therapy," he had emphasized. Lenny understood that unresolved trauma could hold people back and keep them from thinking clearly. He couldn't help but add a touch of humor to his essay, noting that therapists were the only people you could sue for revealing your deepest secrets. The concept of leadership also weighed heavily on his mind. "For one to be a leader, they must have integrity, respect, and humility," he had written. Lenny believed that true leaders were those who sought to uplift those around them, providing opportunities for growth and empowerment. He recognized that the desire for dominance over others often hindered genuine leadership. As Lenny continued to absorb the wisdom shared in his English Composition Course, he felt a renewed sense of purpose. The power of words, of communication, of understanding the human mind—it was all coming together in his mind. And so, he continued his journey of self-discovery and learning, knowing that the never-ending story of his life was filled with lessons yet to be uncovered. Lenny's exploration of Stokely Carmichael's philosophy and the broader context of social justice had ignited a fire within him, deepening his understanding of the world and his place in it. As he sat in his classes at Morehouse College, the ideas he encountered continued to shape his perspective on life, society, and the human condition. He contemplated the significance of the Black Power Movement and its call for "cultural, political, and economic self-determination." The movement, which had its roots in the African American community, inspired Lenny with its message of empowerment and self-acceptance. The phrases "We have to stop being ashamed of being black" and "Black is Beautiful" resonated with him, reinforcing the importance of embracing one's identity and heritage. In his pursuit of knowledge, Lenny couldn't help but draw connections between personal empowerment and entrepreneurship. He believed that the ability to control one's actions stemmed from the power of one's mind. Too often, individuals placed themselves in situations that were detrimental to their well-being because they allowed negative thoughts to consume them. Lenny recognized that the mind was a potent force, capable of shaping one's destiny. He also delved into the influence of external factors on individual actions and thoughts. The societal and economic pressures that weighed on people, coupled with the negative influences they encountered, had profound effects. Lenny mused that losing sight of oneself often meant losing control over one's actions, a sobering thought that underscored the importance of self-awareness and mental resilience. As his studies continued, Lenny turned his attention to the complex relationship between religion and politics in America. He acknowledged that the combination of these two forces had played a significant role in shaping the nation. Religion, with its power and discipline, had been used as a tool for influencing the masses and instilling core values in society. This connection between religion and morality intrigued him, as both systems aimed to regulate human behavior and interactions. Lenny was particularly fascinated by the influence of religion on the Constitution of the United States. The document bore the marks of religious influence, from the national anthem to the currency. The freedom of religion, enshrined in the First Amendment, was a powerful testament to the country's commitment to diversity and tolerance. He also explored the ever-evolving landscape of technology and social media, recognizing the profound impact it had on society. Lenny saw how the constant sharing of personal information had become the norm, shaping collective beliefs and trends. He believed that in this digital age, people needed to question the direction in which society was headed, and the parallels between their own lives and the world they lived in. In one of his musings, Lenny contemplated the concept of a Babylonian hero. He dissected the idea, highlighting that heroes, even in the grandeur of their deeds, were still human at their core. He examined the transformation of Gilgamesh from a powerful but morally flawed figure to a hero with human emotions. It was through the pain of defeat and the experience of compassion that Gilgamesh's true heroic qualities emerged. He recognized the value of humility in leadership, noting that true leaders understood the complexities of human nature and the importance of necessary evils. Lenny pondered the idea that life could only thrive when individuals allowed a higher power, whether internal or external, to guide their actions and decisions. Lenny's journey of discovery and self-reflection continued as he delved into the nature of truth and belief. He grappled with the philosophical concept that truth hinged on alignment with reality and the individual's perception of reality. He was acutely aware that the meanings of words and phrases in context played a crucial role in understanding the intricate tapestry of truth. As Lenny's mind expanded and his understanding deepened, he remained committed to his pursuit of knowledge and self-improvement. Morehouse College had become the crucible in which his thoughts, ideas, and beliefs were forged, and he looked forward to the many more chapters that lay ahead in his never-ending quest for wisdom and enlightenment. Lenny's journey through college was marked by his unwavering commitment to self-improvement and his dedication to becoming a positive force in his community. He understood that hard work, when coupled with a well-thought-out strategy, would yield a return on investment. Lenny's perspective on recognition was mature and forward-thinking, emphasizing the importance of focusing on the journey rather than seeking immediate applause. His approach to building a team was grounded in research and mentorship. Instead of chasing the elusive idea of a perfect team, he believed in nurturing and educating those around him, sharing the knowledge and skills required for success. Lenny recognized the strength that came from unity, echoing the sentiment that it takes a village to achieve greatness. Lenny's commitment to personal growth and healing while pursuing success was a testament to his wisdom. He understood that the pursuit of financial freedom and impact was a lifelong journey, one that required a strong foundation of well-being. His mantra of "Anything is possible" echoed the importance of belief and self-confidence. Lenny encouraged others to fall in love with the process of their endeavors, to create exit plans that allowed them to enjoy the fruits of their labor, and to value the journey over the end result. Lenny's involvement in transformative leadership during high school had already instilled in him the importance of voicing societal concerns that were often deemed inappropriate. He recognized the power of like-minded individuals coming together to effect change. His decision to attend a Historically Black College or University (HBCU) was a conscious choice to be in an environment that celebrated and empowered individuals who looked like him. Lenny felt a responsibility to unite and uplift his community, inspired by the need to counteract the oppressive educational process highlighted by Carter G. Woodson. Lenny's journey in college was not solely about acquiring a degree but finding his true self and becoming a resource for his community. He aspired to restore hope and provide keys to success for others, motivated by the desire to be a voice for the voiceless. His experience with DECA and entrepreneurship in high school had ignited his passion for founding and creating opportunities. Lenny understood the importance of timing, patience, perseverance, and self-discipline in his journey towards entrepreneurship. He believed that every individual was the author of their own story, with each day representing a new page and each year a new chapter. Lenny encouraged others not to let their dreams fade away and to recognize the purpose within them. Lenny's contemplation of faith, interpretation, and the theological template highlighted his deep thinking and philosophical nature. He understood the power of faith in connecting unrelated concepts and forging meaning. His thoughts on family and singleness reflected a concern for the evolving dynamics of modern society. Lenny recognized the importance of strong family structures and the role they played in shaping individuals and society. In his pursuit of success, Lenny emphasized the importance of being present, understanding the environment, and following guidelines and procedures. He treated his education as a job and believed in the value of discipline and self-awareness. Lenny's journey through college was a testament to his growth, wisdom, and commitment to making a positive impact on the world. He recognized the power of education, mentorship, and community in shaping his path toward success and self-discovery. Truth, a concept that has fascinated philosophers and thinkers throughout history, is a complex and multifaceted idea. It is the cornerstone of our understanding of reality and the basis for our communication with one another. In its essence, truth is a series of sentences or statements that align with reality. When we say something is true, we are essentially claiming that it corresponds to the way things are. This alignment with reality is crucial for effective communication and understanding among individuals. P.F. Strawson and Gareth Evans, two prominent philosophers, have delved into the nature of truth and belief. They agree that a statement is true if, and only if, it accurately represents the state of affairs in the world. Similarly, a belief is considered true if it aligns with the way the believer perceives the world. Language plays a fundamental role in our ability to convey truth. Without language, we would struggle to express our thoughts and share our understanding of the world. Language is the medium through which we communicate our beliefs and truths to others. It allows us to express our thoughts and be understood by those around us. It's essential to recognize that a statement is not false merely because it lacks a specific detail or because it includes the phrase "it is true." The validity of a statement is determined by its alignment with reality. Truth should not be accepted at face value but should be subjected to scrutiny and questioning until its validity is established. Truth can be viewed in two primary senses: the primary sense, which pertains to the way things actually are, and the extended sense, which includes beliefs and statements that may not have a direct reference to the real world. Evans extends the concept of truth to include statements that are not necessarily tied to concrete objects or events but may relate to abstract or future beliefs. Ultimately, truth is a complex interplay of language, belief, and reality. It is a fundamental concept that underpins our understanding of the world and our ability to communicate effectively. While philosophers may continue to explore its intricacies, truth remains an essential aspect of human cognition and communication. Lamarr's journey from a young boy charged with taking care of his family by his great-grandfather to a determined and passionate young man with a clear sense of purpose is truly remarkable. His story reflects the struggles and challenges that many Black individuals face in society, but it also showcases the resilience and determination to overcome obstacles. As a fourth-generation grandchild, Lamarr felt the weight of responsibility to keep his family together and close despite the disagreements and separations that often occur within families. He understood the importance of embracing his identity and uniqueness as a Black individual and saw it as a gift rather than a curse. Lamarr's sense of purpose evolved over the years, from aspiring to various careers to eventually realizing his calling as a change agent through music and spoken word. He understood the power of music to influence society positively and saw it as a way to plant a positive impact on many lives. His experiences in high school, especially his Senior Project, taught him valuable lessons about time management, perseverance, and creativity under pressure. Lamarr's passion for music and his desire to be a part of the music industry fueled his determination to succeed in this field. Throughout his journey, Lamarr faced challenges and obstacles, but he never allowed them to define his future. He recognized the importance of trusting his intuition, stepping out of his comfort zone, and building a strong network to achieve his goals. Lamarr's story is a testament to the power of self-discovery, resilience, and determination. He is on a path to fulfill his life's purpose and make a positive impact on the world, particularly in addressing issues like "The Delmar Divide" and advocating for change within the African-American community. His journey is an inspiring example of how one individual can strive to be a catalyst for positive change in society. Lenny Speaks was a student at Morehouse College, and his passion for music was undeniable. He wasn't your typical student leader in the traditional sense, but his influence on campus was undeniable. Lenny was a playlist curator, and he had a resonated deeply with Lenny. He believed in the importance of helping others and providing support with honesty, integrity, fairness, and, when needed, teamwork. When something went wrong, people turned to those with the skills and abilities to fix the problems. Lenny saw himself as a service provider, ready to lend a helping hand when needed. Love was another profound concept that Lenny contemplated. He recognized that love was a force of nature that could control a person's actions. However, he also understood the complexity of love. People often hurt those they loved, not out of malice but due to temptation, a lack of attention, or a failure to express affection. Love was a beautiful yet sometimes painful journey. As he continued to ponder his future, Lenny thought about his role as a bridge between his community and the wider world. His aspirations were shaped by a spiritual foundation and the desire to inspire others to find their purpose. He believed in the power of knowledge and networking to uplift his community, and he wanted to bridge the gap between African-Americans and the opportunities they deserved. Lenny's time at Morehouse College was essential in shaping his path. He aimed to graduate with a degree in Sociology, a foundation for his future endeavors. Beyond education, he saw the value in building a network of like-minded individuals who shared his vision for change. He recognized that it would take a collective effort to make a real impact. As he prepared to embark on his journey, Lenny was determined not to lose sight of his roots. He understood that knowing one's history and identity was crucial for both personal growth and building a stronger community. He embraced the idea of being the voice for the voiceless, a source of hope and inspiration. Now, in his college dorm room at Morehouse, Lenny Speaks was not just a dreamer; he was a young man with a vision, armed with the knowledge, ambition, and determination to chase his dreams and create a better world for his community and generations to come. Lenny Speaks sat in his dorm room, surrounded by the mementos of his journey so far. His path had been marked unique talent for using music to bring people together and uplift their spirits during times of crisis. Leadership, to Lenny, was not about holding a formal position or title. Instead, it was about what he could do to assist those around him in staying afloat, especially during challenging times. He believed in the power of music to heal, inspire, and unite. Lenny understood that leadership was rooted in integrity, respect, and humility, and he embodied these qualities in everything he did.Lenny's playlist curation wasn't just about putting together a random collection of songs. It was an art form to him—a way to be a bridge over troubling waters for his fellow students. During times of stress, exams, or personal struggles, Lenny would create playlists that resonated with the emotions of his peers. His carefully selected songs had the power to provide comfort, motivation, or a moment of joy when it was needed most. He wasn't just leading by example; he was serving as the tail, ensuring that those who were initially following him didn't fall behind. Lenny's leadership was about getting others to do something they wanted to do, not because they had to but because they were inspired to do so by the music he curated. Lenny often quoted Mahatma Gandhi, believing in the mantra of being the change he wanted to see in the world. He recognized that everyone had a purpose, and his was to plant a positive impact on as many lives as possible through music. In addition to curating playlists, Lenny was dedicated to building a voice for the voiceless. He used his talent to highlight important social issues and inspire change. His playlists were not just a collection of songs but a narrative that conveyed powerful messages about unity, justice, love, and hope. Despite not holding a traditional leadership position, Lenny's influence on campus was undeniable. He connected with individuals through his music, and he was actively involved in extracurricular activities, including organizing events that brought people together through music and dialogue. As he matured, Lenny continued to grow and develop his skills. He learned how to balance his time effectively, honing his entrepreneurial spirit. He also embarked on a journey of self-discovery, understanding himself better and using that knowledge to connect with others. Lenny's ability to network effectively with those who shared his dedication to positive change allowed him to expand his influence beyond the campus. He collaborated with musicians, activists, and community leaders, amplifying the impact of his playlists and advocacy. Throughout his collegiate journey, Lenny never settled for anything less than what he believed he was worth. He learned from his past mistakes and used them as stepping stones toward a brighter future. In the end, Lenny Speaks might not have fit the conventional mold of a student leader, but he embodied the essence of leadership in his own unique way. Through the power of music, his playlists sparked change, inspired action, and united a community during both good times and bad. Lenny's legacy at Morehouse College was one of unconventional leadership, where a passion for music became a beacon of hope and inspiration for all who had the privilege of listening. Lenny Speaks was a student leader at Morehouse College, although it seemed like nobody had recognized his full potential. Lenny was a young man with a unique gift that set him apart from his peers. He was a playlist curator. In an era where music had become the soundtrack to many people's lives, Lenny had mastered the art of creating playlists that could convey emotions, tell stories, and transport the listener to different worlds. Yet, despite his remarkable talent, Lenny's leadership often went unnoticed. He lived by the belief that leadership wasn't just about holding a position or title; it was about making a positive impact on those around him. He held fast to the values of integrity, respect, and humility, always seeking to lead by example. Lenny saw his role as more than just creating playlists. He believed in being a bridge over the troubling waters of life, providing solace and inspiration to those who needed it through his carefully crafted musical journeys. He understood that leadership meant serving as the tail, ensuring that those who followed him were not left behind. However, the world around him didn't seem to grasp the significance of his work. In a college where traditional leadership roles were highly visible and often emphasized, Lenny's quiet yet impactful leadership was often overshadowed. Lenny often found inspiration in the words of great leaders like Dwight D. Eisenhower, Mahatma Gandhi, and Tupac Shakur. Their wisdom fueled his belief that he could be the spark that would change the world, albeit in his unique way. He understood that being a voice for the voiceless could transform societies and that music had the power to convict those who had become menaces to society. Through his extracurricular activities in school, church, and the community, Lenny had developed an understanding of the responsibilities that leaders should possess. He wasn't a supervisor or a manager, but he was an overseer, working quietly to better those around him. Lenny was determined to expand his influence on the Morehouse College campus. He set out to establish relationships with as many students and faculty as possible throughout the entire Atlanta University Center (AUC). He wanted to showcase the three factors of leadership: integrity, respect, and humility through his interactions and the music he curated. As he matured, Lenny's vision expanded. He sought wisdom and knowledge through a variety of experiences, aiming to learn how to balance his time effectively. He was not content with just being a playlist curator; he aspired to become an entrepreneur, someone who could create opportunities for others while staying true to his values. Additionally, Lenny was on a journey of self-discovery. He knew that understanding himself on a deeper level was essential to becoming a more effective leader. And last but not least, he was keen on networking with those dedicated to building a successful future, recognizing that together, they could achieve so much more. Throughout his collegiate journey, Lenny was unwavering in his commitment to not settle for anything less than he was worth. He learned from his past mistakes and aimed to lead by example, not just with words but with his actions. Lenny Speaks might not have fit the traditional mold of a student leader, but he was quietly changing lives, one playlist at a time, and his potential as a creative leader was slowly but surely being recognized. Lenny, a bright and charismatic student at Morehouse College, was known for his intellectual curiosity and his love for weaving words into intriguing stories. One day, he found himself seated in the bustling campus library, engrossed in a series of articles about the complexities of eye contact in humans and animals. As he pored over the research, his attention was drawn to a mysterious woman sitting a few tables away. She had an air of enigmatic charm about her, and her eyes held a captivating depth that instantly intrigued Lenny. He couldn't resist the temptation to impress her with his newfound knowledge, all while maintaining her anonymity. Lenny decided to engage her with a riddle, drawing inspiration from the Bible verse Proverbs 3:15, which spoke of wisdom being more precious than rubies. With a sly smile and a twinkle in his eye, The woman looked up, her gaze fixing on Lenny. "Hello," she replied, her eyes locked onto his, the intrigue mutual. Lenny decided to start with the riddle. "You know, I've been pondering over the precious gems of wisdom and the secrets hidden in plain sight. There's a verse in Proverbs 3:15 that says, 'She is more precious than rubies; nothing you desire can compare with her.' Isn't it fascinating how some truths can be right in front of us yet remain shrouded in mystery?" The woman nodded, her curiosity piqued. "Indeed, wisdom can be elusive, even though it's often right before our eyes." Emboldened by her response, Lenny continued his subtle quest to impress her. "Much like the hidden treasures of wisdom, the world of communication has its mysteries, too. I was reading about the intricate dance of eye contact among humans, vertebrates, and even invertebrates. It's as though seeing is believing for some, while others find it deceptive." As he spoke, Lenny delved into the articles he had been reading. He shared insights about the significance of eye contact in human nonverbal communication, mentioning the varied experiments conducted to measure eye contact and even the role of observer bias. He explained the differences in eye contact behavior between humans, dogs, and fiddler crabs, drawing parallels with how these species used their eyes for survival and connection. The woman was captivated by Lenny's knowledge and his unique approach to conversation. She followed his words closely, her own eyes reflecting a growing connection between them. Lenny finally reached the part where he presented his own experiment on gender and eye contact. "You know," he said, "I conducted a small study to understand whether gender influences our ability to maintain prolonged eye contact. It was fascinating. In the end, I found that there's indeed a correlation, but I won't reveal more. Sometimes, it's the enigma that makes life more interesting." The woman smiled, her eyes glinting with intrigue. "You have a way with words, Lenny. I can't help but wonder what other mysteries you hold." Lenny chuckled, keeping her name and identity shrouded in the riddles of their conversation. "Ah, life is full of mysteries, and I believe some are meant to be uncovered one riddle at a time." Their conversation continued, a dance of words, riddles, and unspoken connection. The woman remained a mystery to Lenny, but he had made an unforgettable impression by combining wisdom, riddles, and the magic of conversation, proving that sometimes the most captivating stories are those that are never fully revealed. Lenny Speaks, a young and enthusiastic music enthusiast, found himself on a journey through time and music as he delved into the works of the legendary Quincy Jones. His admiration for Quincy Jones grew over time as he discovered the maestro's ability to bridge the past with the present, creating timeless music that transcended generations. Despite being born in a different era, Lenny felt a deep connection with Quincy's work. One day, as Lenny immersed himself in Quincy Jones' albums, he had a vision. It was as if time itself had bent, and he found himself transported to a realm where he could interact with the musical genius he so greatly admired. In his vision, Lenny stood in a dimly lit recording studio. Instruments of various kinds were scattered around, and the air was thick with the sweet scent of nostalgia. He watched in awe as Quincy Jones, the man himself, orchestrated a mesmerizing piece of music. Quincy turned to Lenny, his eyes filled with wisdom and a mischievous spark. "You're here to see how the magic happens, young man," he said with a grin. Lenny nodded, barely able to contain his excitement. "I've always admired your work, Mr. Jones. Your ability to blend genres and create timeless music is truly inspiring." Quincy chuckled, his laughter like a melody. "Well, my boy, music is all about pushing boundaries and breaking the rules, but it's also about respecting the greats who came before us. You see, I've always believed in bridging the past with the present. That's what makes music resonate with people across generations." As Quincy shared his insights, the studio filled with an eclectic mix of musicians, each an icon in their own right. Herbie Hancock's fingers danced across the keys, and Stevie Wonder's soulful voice filled the room. Michael Jackson, in his prime, stood in the corner, a shy yet mesmerizing presence. Quincy Jones began to conduct the musicians, and the room erupted with a symphony of sounds. Lenny watched in awe as they created a harmonious fusion of jazz, pop, and R&B. Each note was a testament to Quincy's genius, his ability to craft music that transcended time and genre. Throughout the vision, Lenny realized that Quincy's music wasn't just a combination of notes and rhythms; it was a bridge connecting people, eras, and genres. His work was a testament to the power of collaboration and the celebration of the great musicians who had paved the way. As the music swirled around him, Lenny couldn't help but feel a profound connection to the world of music, to the artists who had left an indelible mark on the industry. And, in that moment, he understood Quincy Jones's philosophy that great music is a timeless gift to humanity, meant to be celebrated and shared. The vision slowly faded, and Lenny returned to his reality, deeply inspired by his encounter with the musical maestro. He knew that the lessons he had learned in that transcendent experience would shape his own journey in the world of music. Quincy

Jones had not only created masterpieces but had also passed on the torch of inspiration to the next generation. Lenny was determined to carry that torch forward, embracing the past, present, and future of music with a heart full of passion.

Chapter IV: The Struggle

In a moment of profound self-reflection, a person received a cascade of wisdom from the depths of their subconscious mind. It was as though a wellspring of understanding had opened up within them, and they couldn't help but be awestruck by the depth of insight that unfolded. They understood that, as Black individuals, the challenge wasn't so much about accessing capital but about the choices made to obtain it. The wisdom illuminated the path to closing the wealth gap, emphasizing the importance of investing not only in "Black Owned Businesses" but also in themselves, their friends, and their loved ones within the community they grew up in. This torrent of wisdom conveyed a simple yet powerful process: identify the problem, then methodically run a diagnostic test to uncover the solution. It was a call to action that encouraged them to focus on finding practical resolutions to their challenges. They were urged to shift their perspective away from the mere celebration of holidays and, instead, utilize those moments to express gratitude for their journey and their very existence. This wisdom urged them to recognize that life is a precious gift, even when time feels limited and the pace of life is frantic. The importance of relationships was emphasized. Instead of seeking ways to eliminate intermediaries, they should work on building solid connections and establish mutually beneficial ways to profit. The middleman was portrayed as the essential adhesive that held everything together. The wisdom underscored the power of visualization and the importance of setting and achieving one's goals. The person felt a deep sense of accomplishment as they realized they had followed through with everything they had committed to up to that point. It was a testament to the importance of healing along the way, ensuring they could savor the fruits of their labor once they reached their goals. They were encouraged not to be disheartened by a lack of recognition, as the audience's applause was meant to come at the end of the show. The wisdom advised them to cultivate contentment even when circumstances did not align with their expectations. The concept of legacy was depicted as a reflection of one's beliefs and values. Regardless of life's challenges, the wisdom revealed that the essence of humanity lay in natural instincts, love, shared tears, the pain of struggle, and the tranquility that bestowed happiness. The message highlighted the unpredictability of life, whether it be in the form of a written page, a movie, a song, a quote, a loved one, or even a simple plate of rice. The person's ultimate goal was to master themselves, understanding that their soul held more value than any external riches. The wisdom illuminated the unexpected power that lay within the complexion of their skin, acknowledging the importance of their actions and their voice. In the realm of political representation, wisdom emphasized the need for equality and descriptive representation. It acknowledged that some political parties were more committed to promoting the voices of women, understanding that representation should mirror the constituents themselves. The wisdom then turned to cherished memories, stressing the importance of retaining the joy of laughter, even as those moments turned into distant memories. It reminded them that while everyone loved the sunshine, the rain had its own beauty and purpose. The lesson concluded by acknowledging the lessons of family, recognizing that wisdom and guidance often came from unexpected sources. It encouraged the person to stay in their lane and remain focused, all while remaining aware of the world around them. Lenny Speaks found himself in deep thought, contemplating the intricacies of language and meaning. He mused, "We don't learn the meaning of a new sentence independently. The point is, we don't need to do this." It occurred to him that like truth, language required the participation of at least two parties to be both true and understood. One party had to comprehend the meanings of the relevant nouns, conjunctions, and predictions and effectively express their understanding of semantics by constructing a series of sentences. Lenny pondered further, "The object of semantics isn't to explain the ordinary speaker's mastery of a limitless range of sentences, their grasp of meaning, and their logical relations." He realized that proof was not always a necessity; sometimes, providing an explanation aligned with what was true was sufficient. In a sense, it was more about an analogical extension of forms rather than delving into semantic contents beyond their primary applications. The importance of consciousness in understanding language became apparent to Lenny. He acknowledged that language was closely tied to the mind, and as thinkers, individuals needed to be attentive and present to comprehend how language and semantics functioned. Using language and semantics appropriately, especially in arguments, was crucial for effective communication. The speaker had to present their thoughts clearly for the observer to understand. Lenny recognized the value of hard work and a strategic approach, understanding that they would yield a return on investment. He encouraged not to fret if recognition didn't come immediately, as the applause was meant for the end of the show—this was just the beginning. Instead of seeking the perfect team, Lenny advised researching the requirements of the roles sought to be filled and teaching family and friends the secrets to success in those roles. It truly took a village. Healing while pursuing financial success was equally crucial to enjoy the fruits of labor once the bag was secured—a lifestyle of financial freedom, gratitude, limitless possibilities, and impact. Lenny's thoughts continued to inspire as he declared that anything was possible, urging all to believe and never allow anyone to dim their light. He stressed the importance of making time for what one truly desired and falling in love with the process more than the highlights. Creating an exit plan was essential to fully enjoy the life one had built for themselves and their loved ones. He reminded everyone that it wasn't a race, and they should go at their own pace, as the journey was often more significant than the end result itself. Lenny emphasized self-worth, knowing that one had to believe they belonged before getting into any significant position. He acknowledged that not everyone would understand their vision, but he encouraged the understanding that everyone was somebody to somebody. He reminisced about his time in high school, where he had joined Transformative Leaders, a group that allowed students to have their voices heard on societal issues often considered inappropriate to discuss. He recognized the importance of building connections with like-minded individuals, understanding that it was crucial to act as change agents and unite for a common purpose. His choice to attend a Historically Black College or University was rooted in the desire to surround himself with those who looked like him. He felt a strong sense of unity within the Black community and aspired to be an influence in uniting them for a cause he believed in, similar to Dr. King's intentions. He recalled the impact of education on one's perception of themselves and their race and understood the importance of empowering the Black community to rise above historical narratives. If we were never taught hate, the prejudices of the world would not exist. Lenny Speaks, with his thoughtful and introspective mind, found himself reflecting on various aspects of life and relationships. He saw relationships as a balance between assets and liabilities, understanding the importance of making everyone feel valued, like they were the number one draft pick on his roster. Lenny's insights into dating were equally profound, emphasizing the need to understand a person's vibes by getting to know them deeply. He encouraged fellow men to embrace chivalry and consistency, showing that thoughtful gestures like matching flowers to a woman's Instagram feed could leave a lasting impression. Lenny believed that the amount of money spent on a date didn't necessarily equate to the best experience; it was more about planning a date that aligned with the person's personality and interests. Cultural appreciation versus appropriation was another topic Lenny delved into. He stressed the importance of respecting and appreciating different cultures when adapting to them, rather than appropriating them.

Lenny believed that everyone should contribute positively to the culture they were embracing. His thoughts also touched on the role of women in society and their impact on men. He recognized that women played a significant role in shaping men's lives and the world at large. He acknowledged the influence of strong women like Afeni Shakur and Stacey Abrams, who had made remarkable contributions to society. Lenny didn't shy away from discussing the influential figures of the past, such as Dr. Martin Luther King Jr. and Malcolm X, and their impact on the Civil Rights Movement. He emphasized the commonalities between these leaders, despite their different approaches, and the need for unity in pursuing justice. Lenny's personal journey in sharing his art and poetry on platforms like Instagram showcased his growth and the power of self-expression. He realized the influence he could have on others and appreciated the platform for connecting with people and sharing his creative works. Through his introspective musings, Lenny Speaks touched on a wide range of topics, from relationships and dating to culture, the role of women, and the legacies of influential leaders. His perspective offered valuable insights into navigating life's complexities and striving for unity and positive change in the world. I remember that day like it was yesterday. The day I decided to share my granny's cooking with the birds. It might sound strange, but it was a turning point in my life, a moment that set me on a path I never could have predicted. I grew up in South Saint Louis, a place where life had its challenges, especially for a young African American like me. But my granny, she was a beacon of light in my world. She had this magical ability to turn the simplest ingredients into the most delicious meals. Her kitchen was my sanctuary, a place where I learned the power of food to bring people together. After graduating from McCluer North High School, I had the opportunity to attend Morehouse College. It was a dream come true for me, a chance to escape the limitations of my hometown and pursue my passion for creating positive change. I knew I wanted to make a difference in St. Louis, a city divided by what they called the Delmar Divide, a term that describes the stark segregation and inequality that existed there. My upbringing in church had instilled in me a sense of purpose, a belief that we all have a calling. And I felt that my calling was to create experiences, opportunities, and help others find their path. During my college journey, I set my sights on creating an innovative art space, a place where people could seek opportunities in careers they were passionate about, learn to make a living, and become financially literate. I believed that African Americans, who contributed so much to the labor and economics of this country, should not be suffering from poverty, lack of resources, and opportunities. It was time to change that narrative, to empower our community to believe in themselves and their worth. But I also knew that to address these social issues, we needed to have a sociological imagination. We needed to connect our personal troubles with the larger societal problems. The Delmar Divide was a glaring example of legal segregation that plagued our city. It was like taking half of Bankhead and half of Buckhead and placing them on the same street. Our society had romanticized power and struggle, even though they didn't mix. We needed to redefine what happiness and satisfaction meant, to shift our focus from what was destructive to what was necessary. And we needed to challenge gender roles, to recognize that women could lead just as effectively as men. My mother played a crucial role in shaping my values and outlook on life. She taught me the importance of education and not underestimating the value of learning. She instilled in me the essence of never being jealous, of having the heart to know what I wanted in life. She taught me to identify the strength of a strong black woman. But there was also someone else who had a profound impact on my life, someone I affectionately called "Caramel Cake." She taught me how to love through imperfections, how to submit for the right reasons, and how to understand the struggles and sorrows of women. She was my muse, and our connection was deeper than I could have imagined. My journey through college wasn't without its challenges. I struggled with a statistics class, and my pride got in the way. But it was also a time of growth and self-discovery. I learned that forgiveness was essential, that we should forgive our loved ones for their imperfections and mistakes. Attending a Historically Black College or University (HBCU) opened my eyes to the systemic issues facing the black community. We faced low expectations, poor advisement, and a lack of quality education in our high schools. These factors were detrimental to our community's growth. But I believed that change was possible, that we could unite and invest in our communities. Black Americans had built this country, and it was time to invest in our future. We needed to overcome our egocentrism and support each other's success. But it also had its downsides, as it perpetuated unrealistic ideals and standards. The media's portrayal of the "ideal woman" had led to medical issues and unhealthy behaviors. We needed to question our direction and the society we lived in, to strive for a "perfect world" where happiness was based on what was necessary, not destructive. But we also needed to take responsibility for our actions and choices. We couldn't be reactive; we had to be proactive in addressing the challenges we faced as a society. Only by uniting and holding ourselves accountable could we achieve real growth. My time at Morehouse had its ups and downs, but it was a transformative experience. I had the privilege of meeting people, who later became my big brothers and mentors. He saw something in me, even when I had a chip on my shoulder. It was during this time that I began working on initiatives like The Brown Street Connection and 50 Candles, projects aimed at connecting students with alumni and studying abroad programs. I also dreamed of starting a country club, The Dystrct, similar to The Gathering Spot, where people could work, collaborate, and unwind. I believed in simplifying the process and creating spaces where people could come together, share their truths, and make a difference. Believe it or not, women are "the good thing." Even says it in the Holy Bible. Women are therapists, lawyers, doctors, and everything you need and more. All you have to do is unlock that side of her. Lenny Speaks was a man whose name didn't carry much weight beyond his own circle. He was an unassuming figure in a world of voices clamoring for attention. Lenny was a thinker, a doer, and a person who believed in the power of community. He had grown up in a neighborhood where opportunities were scarce, but he never let that define him. He understood that, as a Black man, the challenge wasn't just about getting access to capital; it was about how they went about it. Lenny had a philosophy that he often shared with anyone who would listen. He believed that closing the wealth gap required more than just investing in "Black Owned Businesses." It meant investing in themselves, their friends, and their loved ones within the community they grew up in. Lenny's approach was simple: identify the problem, run a diagnostic test, and seek out the solution. He was a firm believer that the true meaning of holidays was often lost in the rush to celebrate. Lenny saw these moments as opportunities to extend gratitude for how far one had come. He believed in expressing gratitude for simply being alive because, in the grand scheme of things, life was a precious gift. Time was fleeting, and it was vital to appreciate life itself, both before and after it became a task at hand. Lenny also understood the importance of building relationships. He saw middlemen not as obstacles but as the glue that brought everything together. Instead of trying to cut them out, he advocated for creating relationships that benefited all parties involved. To him, it was a matter of cooperation over competition. Throughout his life, Lenny had meticulously written out his goals, and he had an impressive track record of achieving them. He knew the value of healing along the way, ensuring that when he reached his end goal, he could enjoy the fruits of his labor. Lenny didn't concern himself with the recognition he received along the way; he understood that the audience was supposed to clap at the end of the show. He had learned to find contentment even when things didn't go his way. For Lenny, one's legacy was a reflection of what they believed in and stood for. Regardless of life's challenges, he believed that their natural instincts were what bound people together. Love, tears, pain, and peace were all part of what brought them solace. Lenny had a message that he was passionate about. He reminded people not to disrespect women and to remember that it was their mothers who brought them into the world. He believed in the interconnectedness of humanity and that every individual had a role to play in creating a better world. Lenny's perspective on life was unique. He saw it as a journey filled with unexpected directions. Whether it was through a book, a movie, a song, a quote, a loved one, or a simple plate of rice, he aimed to master himself. He knew that the richness of his soul far exceeded any material wealth. His words resonated deeply, "I never knew the complexion of my skin could hold so much power. I knew actions spoke louder than words, but by the complexion of my skin, I never knew they'd be even louder." Lenny had a clear sense of purpose, and he was unapologetic about it. He knew that life was uncertain, and one's last moments could arrive unexpectedly. But he urged people to follow directions, to seek guidance in real life, and to work together to create a better world. He had a particular passion for addressing the challenges faced by Black communities, especially in the realm of education. Lenny was well-versed in the Social Disorganization Theory and its implications. He believed that one of the key reasons crime rates were high in Black communities was the public-school system's failure to prepare Black youth for life after high school. Lenny explained the various domains of education, highlighting the significance of the Social Domain. He saw the treatment of students based on their social status as a critical issue. He questioned whether students were adhering to stereotypes to be accepted, whether popularity was the only way to receive support from faculty, and whether students were suffering academically due to factors beyond their control. He passionately argued that student-athletes, often admired as public figures, should receive a quality education as a priority. Lenny believed that when students felt unsupported by faculty, it hindered their potential for success. Lenny recognized that the treatment of students by faculty was a significant factor in their educational experience. He explored the impact of factors like the faculty's ability to relate to students, the social status of the student, the relationship between faculty and students, and the role of race and ethnicity in the interaction. Lenny advocated for creating more equitable and supportive educational environments. He also believed that families played a part in the problem by pressuring their children into certain educational paths. Lenny argued that it was essential for Black youth to have the freedom to choose a lifestyle that suited them rather than being forced into one. In Lenny's eyes, the lack of preparation for Black youth upon graduating high school and the failure to provide alternative pathways contributed to the existence of the Social Disorganization Theory. It was a system failure perpetuated by society's segregation-like practices. Lenny's voice may not have been widely known, but it was a voice of wisdom, community, and empowerment. He lived his life as a testament to the principles he preached, and those who listened were forever changed by his words and actions. Lenny Speaks had always been a visionary. As a proud Morehouse College student, he believed in the power of unity, mentorship, and the unwavering commitment to creating a better future for his fellow Men of Morehouse. Lenny saw his college campus as a canvas for a new beginning, and he was about to paint a masterpiece. The Brown Street Connection, an initiative by the Morehouse Pre-Alumni Association, was Lenny's brainchild. He knew it was time to bring local and national alumni back to the college as it began to open up its doors. Lenny envisioned a platform where these esteemed alumni could create pathways for mentorship and provide opportunities for students to showcase a new generation of talent and thought. The mission was clear: to establish an in-house network of all Morehouse Men and Men of Morehouse through an intergenerational experience with a unique focus on leadership identity. The program also aimed to explore modern frameworks that would prepare Men of Morehouse to become distinguished leaders in society. The target audience was a diverse group of Morehouse College students, ranging from creatives to STEM majors. The Brown Street Connection would consist of a series of events, both in person and virtually, to provide students with mentorship and guidance from professionals in their respective fields. Lenny's program was designed to enhance leadership skills through extracurricular experiences, with a focus on professional development, community service, and networking. The program components included masterclasses in various disciplines such as STEM, business, music, film, dance, art, storytelling, and financial literacy. Panel discussions covered topics like "The Value of a Morehouse Man" and "The Art of a Renaissance Man." Workshops addressed leadership, emotional intelligence, resume building, and portfolio development. It was a comprehensive approach to personal and professional growth. The timeline was set to begin in February 2024, with an event titled "Rebirth of the House." Lenny had a full schedule of activities planned, including fireside chats with alumni, networking events for STEM and creative majors, and student showcases. Potential sponsors were already on the radar, including big names like RedBull, Apple, Google, and The Recording Academy. Lenny's enthusiasm and dedication were contagious, and he believed that with the right support, The Brown Street Connection could become a beacon of opportunity and growth for Morehouse College. As Lenny Speaks embarked on this journey, he knew that his vision was not just about creating an event; it was about leaving a legacy. He saw the potential for a new generation of Men of Morehouse to thrive and make a difference in the world. The Brown Street Connection was more than a program; it was a movement, and Lenny was at its forefront, ready to lead his fellow brothers to a brighter future.

Chapter VI: The Candle

Lenny Speaks had always been a man of purpose, and his thoughts, much like the world around him, were complex and layered. He couldn't help but feel the weight of the struggles faced by his people, by his city, and by the world at large. In the absence of his beloved Great-Grandmother, Rebecca Davis, he found solace in the spiritual connection that persisted. Her prayers, her wisdom, her love, all lived on in him. As he walked through life, Lenny carried the torch of a spiritual foundation instilled in him from a young age. The songs in church, the prayers, and the guidance of his elders had shaped him into the man he was becoming. The path to self-assurance was paved with lessons of humility and understanding. He knew he didn't have all the answers, and he didn't want to. It was in embracing the unknown that he found strength. Lenny believed in the power of companionship, understanding that life was a delicate dance of interdependence. He knew that just because he could do it all by himself, it didn't mean he should. It was in unity and collaboration that true progress was made. And as he moved through the world, he aimed to be the flyest person doing it, not for vanity but to show that excellence was possible in all endeavors. The echoes of Dr. Martin Luther King's wisdom resonated in Lenny's soul. King's vision of a world founded on love, of a society that shifted from materialism to humanity, had never been more relevant. Lenny believed that King's dream of unity among all races was not just a dream but a vision of the future that they were all working towards. As Lenny delved into the complexities of the music industry, he understood the power dynamic at play. The control held by a few major record companies was staggering, and the industry was evolving rapidly with technology. But Lenny believed in the potential of artists to shape their own destinies, to tell their stories, and to be heard by many. He saw technology as a tool for empowerment. In the realm of business, Lenny knew that personal and professional relationships were the keys to success. He understood that it was not always about agreeing with someone's views but about finding common ground and negotiating for mutual benefit. He believed in playing the long game and investing in the right individuals to bring about lasting change. But, for Lenny, it all came back to purpose. He saw his role as bridging the gap, bringing people from diverse backgrounds together, and offering opportunities for all. He knew that embracing the past while tackling new obstacles was the way forward. And he believed that the new generation had a voice and answers of their own to contribute to the ongoing story of progress. Lenny Speaks was a man of layers, complexity, and purpose. His journey was one of self-discovery, empowerment, and a deep commitment to his people and his city. He aimed to be the change he wanted to see and to inspire others to do the same. His words were a reflection of the struggles he had witnessed, the wisdom he had gained, and the vision he held for a brighter future. Lenny Speaks was a man of depth and purpose, and as he shared his thoughts, he poured his heart out with passion and conviction. He understood the struggles faced by women, recognizing that their problems often required extra effort to be heard and addressed. The history of strong women who had fought for their rights, like Ida B. Wells, resonated with him. Ida B. Wells, a journalist, abolitionist, and feminist, had dedicated her life to the advancement of women, especially women of color. Lenny was inspired by her commitment to educating and empowering Black women, ensuring they had a voice in politics. Her efforts had paved the way for future generations, and Lenny believed in treating each woman with the respect she deserved. W.E.B. Du Bois, another influential figure in Lenny's thoughts, had spent his life examining the complex issue of the "Negro problem." Du Bois, with his deep insights into race and social issues, had left a lasting impact on Lenny's perspective. Lenny was determined to address the ongoing struggles of Black people, drawing from Du Bois's mission. For Lenny, it wasn't just about equal representation; it was about descriptive representation, where the experiences of constituents were reflected in their representatives. He believed that having the right people on your team could change your trajectory, and Stacey Abrams was a shining example of this. Her tenacity and refusal to accept defeat were qualities that Lenny admired. She showed that it was the "why" behind one's ambitions that truly mattered. Lenny's thoughts on Dr. Martin Luther King Jr. and Malcolm X revealed his nuanced understanding of their contributions. Despite their differences in approach, Lenny saw their shared goal of pursuing equality for Black people. He admired King's focus on love as a force for unity and X's dedication to Black nationalism, both approaches rooted in love and justice. Women held a special place in Lenny's heart, as he recognized their immense impact on society and individuals. From history to economics, women have played pivotal roles. He firmly believed in the power of partnership, in being honest, and in embracing the truth. He understood that behind every great man, there was often a great woman. Lenny also touched on cultural adaptation, a process that could lead to cultural appreciation or appropriation. He saw it as a reflection of conflict theory, where social and economic resources were sources of struggle among different groups. Cultural adaptation required a delicate balance. As Lenny delved into his own journey, he recounted the moment he decided to share his art with the world. His posts on Instagram, from poetry to music, were his way of making a positive impact and connecting with people. He understood the power of social media as a platform for spreading positivity and inspiration. In a world filled with struggle and complexity, Lenny Speaks was a beacon of hope and understanding. His thoughts and words carried the weight of history and the promise of a brighter future. His passion for justice, love, and unity shone through every line he shared with the world. The pursuit of immortality and a lavish lifestyle are common aspirations in the modern world, and Lenny Speaks contemplated the means to achieve these goals. He recognized that breaking criminal records was possible without breaking the law, referring to the rise of organizations like BMF. As he ruminated on opportunities for Black students, he suggested that HBCUs should establish study abroad programs to immerse students in diverse Black cultures at the collegiate level, expanding their horizons and enriching their identities. Lenny emphasized the importance of planning and applying the scientific method to achieve these dreams. Quality, he believed, was a precursor to honor, and he encouraged a methodical approach to success. For Lenny, harmony was the fusion of shared identity and goodwill. He referenced African moral theory, highlighting the need for actions that promoted shared identity based on good will. Morality, he contended, could take on various definitions, depending on cultural and individual perspectives. In his exploration of moral judgments, Lenny underlined the importance of sound reasoning and impartial consideration of each individual's interests. He cautioned against allowing strong emotions to cloud judgment, as it could lead to premature assumptions without considering opposing arguments. Lenny delved into the concept of social support theory, which focused on reducing the likelihood of crime by providing assistance to those who might resort to criminal behavior. He explained that social support acted as a coping resource, helping individuals make rational choices and avoid reckless actions. Karma theodicy was another concept Lenny introduced, linking actions to consequences and acknowledging the role of intent and divine justice. He mentioned that various forms of karma theodicy existed, some involving the concept of the soul and others not. Lenny's discussion on different types of support, such as emotional, instrumental, informational, and appraisal support, emphasized the significance of building strong relationships in modern society. He contended that major accomplishments were seldom achieved alone and often required social support. Lenny delved into historical movements like the Niagara Movement, led by W.E.B. Du Bois, which demanded civil, political, and social rights for African Americans, including equal educational and economic opportunities and the right to vote. He mentioned the Declaration of Principles (DOP) and its significance in setting principles and tasks for achieving racial equality. Lenny also touched on the contrasting views of W.E.B. Du Bois and Booker T. Washington and how their differences affected the Niagara Movement, highlighting the importance of unity within the struggle for racial equality. Lenny Speaks was a thoughtful and contemplative individual, sharing his insights on various topics, from morality to social support, and the historical context of the civil rights movement. His words encouraged critical thinking and reflection on the path to personal and collective success. Lenny sat in his dorm room at Morehouse College, surrounded by the weight of his own ambitions. The room was filled with books, each one brimming with knowledge and the promise of change. He had always been a dreamer, but his time at Morehouse had intensified his desire to make a difference in the world. Lenny reflected on his purpose in life, recognizing that his journey was unique. His identity, as a young Black man with a passion for service and change, set him apart. He knew he had to embrace who he was, even if it meant doing things in an unorthodox way. Conformity was not his path; he was meant for something different, something special. He considered the role of women in society, acknowledging the immense contributions they had made throughout history. Lenny believed that women had been the real drivers of change, often working behind the scenes. "Behind every great man is a great woman," he thought, as he realized the significance of their influence. Lenny's thoughts shifted to leadership. He understood that a leader was not defined by their title but by their ability to inspire and improve the lives of those around them. He believed that women had the potential to lead in various fields, but societal norms and power struggles sometimes hindered this progress. He saw the potential for a new wave of women leaders in the modern world. Service was a core value that

by a series of decisions, each leading him closer to his true calling. In the quiet solitude of his room, he pondered his life's trajectory and how he had come to be where he was today. The learning process for entrepreneurship had started for Lenny in high school, during his time as a member of DECA. The required marketing class introduced him to the world of entrepreneurship, where he was tasked with creating a business plan. He chose to specialize in fashion consulting, realizing the common struggle men face when buying suits. From young adults to middle-aged men, they all needed assistance, and Lenny was there to provide measurements, budgeting options, and a suit catalog. Terell's Closet was more than just a project; it was the start of his entrepreneurial journey. As Lenny conducted research and became a personal stylist, he discovered the power of the marketing industry. The ability to market any product or service was a potent skill. He understood that with the right knowledge and skills, he could attain financial freedom. Terell's Closet had given him the confidence to aim for a chief executive position. But Lenny's passion didn't stop at entrepreneurship. He had found his identity in music and the arts. Music, in all its forms, held an essential place in his heart. Musicians' dedication to mastering their craft inspired him. He saw a parallel between his passion for playing the piano and writing poetry and the journey of someone he admired, Sean "Diddy" Combs. Diddy's rise to success from an unpaid internship at Uptown Records was a testament to what could be achieved through hard work and passion. Diddy's journey was a source of inspiration for Lenny, showing that success required dedication and persistence. Lenny was aware that he didn't need a college degree or a trade certificate to succeed in the music industry. He hadn't come to college for a degree but to discover himself, gain experience, and surround himself with like-minded individuals. He knew that his advancement in the music industry would depend on his performance and networking. His aspiration wasn't just about finding a place in the music industry. It was about creating his path and generating opportunities for others. Versatility was the key, and artists like Drake, who excelled in various roles, were his role models. "In order for you to be successful, it is going to take more than you," a lesson from Jared Arms echoed in his mind. Lenny understood the importance of humility and surrounding himself with those who shared his vision. While music was his passion, a part of his heart also yearned for a career in law. Lenny had a strong desire to impact the world positively. The freedom, happiness, and creativity he found in music also fueled his desire to make a change through the legal system. Balancing a music career while overcoming financial challenges was a challenge faced by many artists. Lenny realized that maintaining a balanced social life was essential for growth in his career. The way he presented himself could open doors to opportunities in the music industry. One of his aspirations was to become a music producer. He knew that success in the industry required mastery and self-discipline. Setting short-term and long-term goals, evaluating his strengths and weaknesses, and persevering through hardships were his tools for success. One of his biggest shortcomings was the inability to trust his intuition, but he was working on it. Lenny had learned to be comfortable with discomfort and had taken on leadership roles, seeking to bring his aspirations into reality. "A music producer oversees the production and development of songs," and he was ready to take on that role. He was aware of the constant changes and competitive advantages in the industry and knew the importance of building a strong network. Graduating from college was not just about personal success for Lenny. It was about creating opportunities for others, especially in the African-American community. He aimed to fight against the systemic injustices that had held back so many, and he was determined to make a difference. The journey was challenging, and at times, he felt discouraged. He had the potential, but opportunities seemed elusive. However, he refused to let statistics define his fate. He knew that he was in the wrong environment and needed to find the right path. High school had been a mixed experience for Lenny. The poor advisement, low expectations, and low-quality education had hindered his growth. However, he had found his passion through performing arts and had become more aware of his calling. Lenny had briefly explored a career in law enforcement during high school, driven by the desire to change the system and ensure justice for all. His experiences in the Law Enforcement Program had taught him valuable skills and introduced him to the complexities of the field. However, he had realized that the systemic issues in law enforcement would not allow him to be the change agent he aspired to be. Senior year of high school had been one of the most stressful periods in his life. The Senior Project had pushed him to the limit. He had faced difficulties with presentations, research, and creativity, but he had persevered. It was a risk and a learning experience that taught him to use the resources available to make the best out of any situation. Lenny's research into his desired career had revealed more about himself than he had expected. His passion for music and the arts was undeniable, and he wanted a career that didn't feel like work. The joy he found in music and the desire to impact lives through it were his driving forces. In the end, Lenny Speaks knew that his journey was far from over. He had a path to pave, dreams to chase, and a commitment to making a difference in the world. He had learned that it wasn't just about where he was going but also how he got there and who he became along the way. In the quiet of his dorm room, Lenny knew that he was on the right track, and he was ready to face whatever challenges lay ahead. Lenny Speaks lay in his dorm room at Brazeal Hall, surrounded by the echoes of his thoughts. The soft glow of the desk lamp was the only source of light in the dimly lit room. The weight of the past and the hopes of the future converged in his mind, creating a profound stillness. As he gazed at the ceiling, he couldn't help but think about the one person who had been a constant guiding presence in his life - his Great-Grandfather, Clyde Davis. The memories of their time together and the wisdom he had imparted lingered in

Lenny's heart like cherished secrets. Lenny's thoughts traveled to a letter he had penned to his beloved Big Daddy at the tender age of nine. He smiled at the simplicity of his words, the faith he had in God's healing, and the deep sense of love he had expressed. That letter, though unread by its intended recipient, had been a testament to the profound connection between them. Clyde Davis had been a man of unwavering love, providing for his family not only in material ways but also in the richness of knowledge and common sense. He had shaped Lenny's character and instilled values that still burned brightly in his heart. Lenny couldn't help but ponder how different life would be if his Great-Grandfather were still alive. The absence of that guiding presence weighed on him, making him feel the full weight of life's challenges. He knew that pressure was the crucible that forged diamonds, but the longing for that guiding hand remained. The only beloved elder left in Lenny's life was his Great-Grandmother. Her dreams of seeing him graduate and build a successful life were now intertwined with his own aspirations. He vowed to make her proud, to bring tears of joy to her eyes as she witnessed his journey from a seed in his mother's womb to the person he was meant to be. Lenny's journey to Morehouse College, a dream since elementary school, had begun with the intention of self-improvement. He thought that working harder and fearing less would lead to success, but he had learned that it wasn't that simple. The complex reality of his world, the challenges he faced as an African American in a country still grappling with racial injustice, weighed on him. He couldn't help but reflect on James Baldwin's words, understanding the rage that often welled up within him in response to the injustices faced by his community. The historical struggles of African Americans in America were not a distant memory but an ongoing battle. In his heart, he yearned for change, for a world where equal opportunities existed for everyone regardless of their skin color. The worn-out narrative of discrimination and inequality had to be rewritten, and he felt a deep calling to be a part of that change.

Revisiting the legacy of Black Owned Businesses was a step in the right direction. It was a bold endeavor, one that came with its challenges, but he felt the time had come to fully embrace the potential of self-reliance and empowerment within his community. Lenny Speaks closed his eyes, his mind filled with determination and hope. The chapter of his life at Morehouse College was just beginning, and he was ready to embrace the challenges, honor the legacy of his Great-Grandfather, and make a difference in the world he had reflected upon so deeply.

Chapter VII: The Beginning

As Lenny sat alone in his room at Morehouse College, a heavy silence enveloped him. The realization of his Great-Grandmother's passing hit him like a tidal wave, and he found himself drowning in grief. He couldn't help but think about the dreams they had shared, the hopes that now seemed to slip away with her. In the quietude of his room, the memories of Granny's unwavering love and support flooded his mind. The image of her wrinkled hands holding his as she had prayed for his well-being was etched in his heart. He could almost hear her voice, filled with warmth and wisdom, as she had guided him through life's challenges. She had seen him grow from a tiny seed in his mother's womb to the young man he had become. Lenny's eyes glistened with unshed tears as he thought about the milestones he had yearned for Granny to witness. Her presence at his graduation, her tears of joy as he walked across the stage, her pride in his success - these were the dreams they had nurtured together. He had wanted to repay her for the love and guidance she had showered upon him. His journey to Morehouse had been a testament to his aspirations and the values Granny had instilled in him. He had believed that success was about working harder and fearing less. But now, in the wake of her passing, he understood that success was not just about personal achievement. It was also about carrying forward the legacy of love and resilience that she had imparted. The room felt emptier than ever as Lenny realized that Granny's tears of joy, the ones he had so desperately wanted to see, could never be. The pain in his heart was palpable, and it was as if a part of his very being had been taken from him. But as the tears welled in his eyes, Lenny remembered something Granny had often said, "In every storm, there's a rainbow waiting to shine." He could almost hear her voice saying those words, her legacy of hope and strength living on within him. Lenny knew he couldn't bring Granny back, but he could honor her memory by striving to become the person she had believed he could be. He could make her proud by embodying the love, wisdom, and strength she had passed on to him. With newfound determination, Lenny wiped away his tears and whispered softly to the empty room, "I'll make you proud, Granny, in every step I take, in every dream I fulfill, and in every tear of joy I bring to this world. You may not be here to see it, but your love will forever light my way." As he spoke these words, a profound sense of peace and purpose washed over Lenny, and he knew that, even in her absence, Granny's spirit would guide him through the journey of life, just as it always had. In the realm beyond life, where time held no sway, Granny watched over her beloved grandson, Lenny. Her voice, like a gentle whisper from the heavens, reached out to him. She knew his heart was heavy, and she longed to comfort him. "Lenny, my sweet boy," Granny's voice carried the wisdom of ages and the warmth of her enduring love. "I see your tears, and I feel the weight of your grief. I want you to know that I'm here with you, even if you can't see me. Life is but a fleeting moment, and our time together on Earth was just one chapter in our eternal journey." Lenny's heart skipped a beat as he felt Granny's presence, her words wrapping around him like a comforting embrace. "You spoke of purpose and the uniqueness of each soul's journey," Granny continued. "And you're absolutely right. Your purpose is as unique as the stars in the night sky. You, my dear, are destined for greatness, not because you conform to the ordinary, but because you dare to be different, to be yourself. That's what makes you shine like a brilliant star in the darkest of nights." Lenny, his tears now mixed with a bittersweet smile, whispered, "I miss you, Granny." "I know, my boy," Granny replied, her voice full of tenderness. "But our connection transcends the boundaries of the physical world. Remember, you carry my love within you, and I am always with you, guiding you, and cheering you on." Granny's words danced through Lenny's soul, filling him with a sense of renewed purpose. The weight of his grief began to lift, replaced by the comfort of knowing that her love and guidance would forever be a part of him. "As for love," Granny's voice took on an ethereal quality, "it is a force of nature, a gift that knows no bounds. Love may not always be returned in the way we hope, but its power lies in the act of giving, not in the expectation of receiving. Love transforms us, makes us better, and it is the light that shines even in the darkest moments of life." Lenny felt an overwhelming sense of peace as Granny's words wrapped around his heart. She had given him the gift of her wisdom, her love, and her undying presence. In that moment, he understood that he was never truly alone, and that he carried within him the legacy of a remarkable woman. With a heart brimming with newfound strength and purpose, Lenny whispered into the ether, "Thank you, Granny. I love you." And in the quiet room, Granny's voice faded, leaving behind the profound sense that love and wisdom transcended the boundaries of life and death. In the depths of his being, Lenny knew that he carried within him the legacy of an extraordinary woman, and he was ready to embrace the unique path she had shown him, no matter where it might lead. Lenny had returned to Morehouse College after a long and unanticipated break. His steps echoed through the hallowed halls of the historic institution. The lush campus that had once felt like a second home was now filled with the anticipation of a fresh start. It had been a challenging journey, with doubts and setbacks along the way, but he was determined to cross the finish line. With only 20 credits left before graduation, the weight of his unfinished business loomed over him. Lenny's path had taken him on a meandering route, one filled with uncertainty, personal growth, and reflection. He'd needed time away to confront the demons of his past, to grapple with his ambitions and the legacy he hoped to leave behind. As he walked past the grand oak trees that had witnessed the dreams of generations of Morehouse Men, Lenny couldn't help but feel a renewed sense of purpose. The responsibility of being a Morehouse Man weighed on him, and he was ready to carry that torch, even if it meant shouldering the burdens of his community. The familiar faces on campus, the echoes of brotherhood in the air, and the call to greatness that resonated through the very bricks of Morehouse filled him with both nostalgia and motivation. He knew he couldn't change the past, but he could shape his future. The lessons he'd learned during his absence were etched deep within his heart. In the classroom, Lenny found himself rekindling his intellectual fire, devouring books and research with a renewed vigor. His professors and peers noticed his transformation, and he felt the warmth of their support and encouragement. The classroom became a place of growth, of discovery, and of preparing for the challenges ahead. But it wasn't just academics that fueled Lenny's determination. It was a burning desire to bridge the divide he had witnessed growing up, the injustices that had weighed heavily on his heart. It was a commitment to give back to his community, to be a beacon of hope in a world that often seemed bleak. Lenny immersed himself in service, reaching out to local communities, volunteering his time, and sharing his knowledge. He understood that being a Morehouse Man meant being a servant-leader, embodying the core values he held dear – honesty, integrity, teamwork, and fairness. As graduation day approached, Lenny couldn't help but reflect on his journey. He had evolved into a young man who saw beyond the confines of his own ambitions. He was no longer just aspiring to be a lawyer, pastor, or recording artist; he aspired to be a catalyst for change in a world that desperately needed it. The night before graduation, Lenny stood on the grounds of Morehouse College, staring at the starlit sky. He felt the weight of history, the legacy of those who had walked these same paths before him. He whispered to the heavens, "I'm ready." His purpose had crystallized, and it was clear as the brightest constellations above. He was here to bridge divides, to give voice to the voiceless, and to build a better future for his community and the world. With the rising sun on graduation day, Lenny walked across the stage, not just as a graduate, but as a symbol of what it meant to evolve, to overcome, and to embrace the power of one's purpose. The applause of his family, friends, and mentors filled the air, but it was the resounding cheers of the Morehouse brotherhood that lifted his spirit to new heights. As he threw his cap into the air, Lenny knew that his journey was just beginning. With the lessons he had learned, the wisdom he had gained, and the purpose that fueled him, he was ready to spark the change he longed to see in the world. Lenny had come a long way since his days at Morehouse College. He had faced the challenges of self-discovery, struggled with the decision to follow his initial dream of becoming a police officer or embrace a different path. It was a journey filled with twists and turns, doubt and resolution, but it had led him to a profound realization. As he stood at the crossroads of his life, Lenny made a decision that would shape his future. He chose to pursue a career far from the one he had initially envisioned. Instead of becoming a police officer, he resolved to make a difference in a different way. Lenny's calling was clear: he would open a country club called "The Dystrct." It was a vision born from his deep understanding of the injustices and divisions that plagued his hometown, St. Louis, Missouri. He was determined to bridge the gaps, bring people together, and create a space where unity and harmony could thrive. The country club was more than just a business venture for Lenny; it was a symbol of hope, a place where people of all backgrounds could come together, break down barriers, and build connections. It would be a sanctuary for those who sought to escape the divisions of society, a place where unity and fellowship would be celebrated. Lenny's decision was a testament to his commitment to creating a better world. He understood that the injustices minorities faced at the hands of law enforcement wouldn't be resolved solely by becoming a police officer. Instead, he believed in holding law enforcement accountable for proper training, ethics, and fair treatment. His pursuit of "The Dystrct" was a powerful message to society. It was a declaration that he would address the root causes of injustice, prejudice, and bias. Lenny had chosen a path that aligned with his values, a path that would make a meaningful impact on his community and the world. In the end, Lenny's journey had taught him that there were many ways to create change, and it didn't always require following the expected or traditional paths. He knew that his pursuit of unity, fairness, and justice would be his life's work, and he was ready to embrace it with open arms. As he embarked on this new chapter of his life, Lenny held the wisdom of his experiences close to his heart. He had learned that true change began from within, and he was determined to be a beacon of light for those who had faced injustices. The legacy he would leave behind wouldn't be defined by a badge, but by the unity and hope he would instill in the hearts of his community. Lenny was ready to open "The Dystrct" and pave the way for a better future. It was a tearful and emotional journey, filled with climax and wisdom, but it was a journey he was proud to embark upon. Lenny had always felt a deep connection to the world around him, especially when it came to the injustices that plagued his hometown, St. Louis, Missouri. The Delmar Divide, as it was known, was a glaring example of a social problem. It represented the stark contrast between privilege and poverty, opportunity and struggle, all existing on the same street. This division was a form of legal segregation, a reflection of the larger issues of racism, discrimination, and bias that persisted in society. As Lenny delved into the complexities of this social problem, he realized that he had a unique calling in life. He believed that he was placed on Earth to be a change agent, someone who could create opportunities and experiences for others and help them find their paths in a world that often seemed stacked against them. His vision was clear: "The Dystrct," a place where minorities could seek opportunities in careers they were passionate about, while also gaining the knowledge to become financially literate. He was determined to break the cycle where Black Americans, who contributed significantly to the labor force and the economy, still suffered from poverty, lack of resources, and limited opportunities. Lenny's sociological imagination was at the forefront of his mission. He understood that personal troubles, such as being denied opportunities due to one's name or appearance, were deeply connected to broader societal issues. He saw that those in power often romanticized their own success while causing destruction to those who had less. He took inspiration from the sociological giants who had come before him, such as W.E.B. Du Bois and Ida B. Wells. These trailblazers had dedicated their lives to fighting against the social problems of their time, and Lenny was ready to follow in their footsteps. The Delmar Divide was just one piece of a larger puzzle, reflecting the deeply rooted problems of society. Cultural adaptation, cultural appreciation, and cultural exchange were all concepts that Lenny recognized as essential in breaking the cycle of prejudice and bias. He aimed to promote appreciation and understanding among different cultures. Lenny knew that social control played a significant role in maintaining the status quo, but he was ready to challenge it. He recognized that technology and surveillance had become instruments of control, but he believed in the power of individuals to stand against this excessive control. As Lenny approached the culmination of his journey, he was filled with ambition and determination. He was ready to open "The Dystrct" and make a difference in his community. His journey was a testament to the power of one person's vision and determination to change the world. The legacy he aimed to leave behind was one of unity, equality, and opportunity. Lenny had been inspired by the Delmar Divide, but he refused to accept it as the status quo. Instead, he was determined to be the change agent he believed he was meant to be, breaking down the barriers that had divided his city for far too long. With his sociological imagination as his guide, Lenny was ready to embark on a new chapter, and he was determined to make a difference. His journey was a testament to the resilience of the human spirit and the power of individuals to create lasting change in a world filled with social problems. Lenny had spent a great deal of time delving into the stories of individuals who had influenced change throughout history. His journey had been filled with lessons about unity, the shared struggles of minorities, and the importance of understanding one's heritage. The conflicts between different racial groups, such as those that occurred during the Watts riots in Los Angeles, had shown Lenny the weight of imaginary competition. These divisions were born out of a false belief that one group was the enemy of another, when in reality, they were all fighting the same battle as minorities. He had studied figures like Malcolm X and Yuri Kochiyama, who had bridged gaps between different communities. Despite their differences, whether it be race or gender, they had come together to seek peace within their own communities. These stories had inspired Lenny to reflect on his own role as a change agent. Lenny understood that the struggles faced by African-Americans, Asian-Americans, and other minority groups were interconnected. He had learned that people needed to look beyond their differences and join forces to fight for a more just and equal society. The influence of individuals like Gandhi on Martin Luther King Jr. had also left a profound impact on Lenny. He recognized that these leaders had shared their knowledge and ideas across cultures and had found ways to incorporate them into their movements. This cross-cultural exchange of ideas had been instrumental in bringing about positive change. The experiences of Yuri Kochiyama and Malcolm X were a testament to the power of understanding one's heritage. They had both embraced their backgrounds and used them as sources of inspiration for their activism. These stories had shown Lenny that knowing where one came from was essential in taking pride in who they were. As Lenny stood on the precipice of his own journey, he carried with him the wisdom of history. He knew that unity among all races and ethnicities was not just a dream but a goal worth pursuing. His ambition was fueled by the lessons he had learned about the power of individuals to create lasting change. He was ready to embrace his heritage, like the leaders who had inspired him, and work towards a better future. Lenny had come to understand that the weight of his past was not a burden but a source of strength, guiding him to curate a brighter future for his community and beyond. As I stood at the crossroads of ambition and adventure, the weight of history pressed heavily on my shoulders. The "color line," a problem that had persisted throughout the twentieth century, had left its mark on the world, affecting people of all races and backgrounds. It was the relation of the darker to the lighter races, a divide that had scarred Asia, Africa, America, and the islands of the sea. Black people had been instrumental in building this country, and their cultures had enriched the tapestry of the world. Yet, they were the ones who suffered the most, facing injustice, resource disparities, and a lack of human rights. It was a bitter irony that the very cultures upon which the world thrived were the ones most oppressed. The concept of integration, once hailed as a means to bridge the gap, had often fallen short of its promise. It seemed to have tainted the access to quality resources and the freedoms that Black people truly deserved. Modern times bore witness to a scarcity of predominantly Black areas functioning well, with Black-owned businesses thriving. The color line, I believed, still lingered in the twenty-first century. It endured due to a collective lack of knowledge regarding the true power we held as a united people. Redlining and gentrification, in particular, remained as stark reminders of the deep-seated racial inequalities. These issues, however, could fade into the background if we as a community reinvested in our own neighborhoods. A simple act of providing knowledge to the next generation could work wonders. I was convinced that the path to overcoming the color line lay in reclaiming our autonomy and self-sufficiency. If we returned to invest in our own communities, if we tackled our problems head-on without relying on anyone else, the very notion of the "color line" would fade away. The power we sought lay within ourselves, in our unity, in our history, and in our determination to forge a better future. And so, I set forth with ambition and adventure as my guides, ready to carry the torch of knowledge, justice, and self-reliance to my people. The challenges of the past would not define our future, for I believed that, united, we could overcome the color line and paint a brighter, more equitable world for generations to come. As I reflect on my journey and the words I've written, I can't help but feel a sense of fulfillment. My path has been filled with challenges, setbacks, and moments of doubt, but it has also been a journey of self-discovery, growth, and resilience. The words I've shared are a testament to the evolution of my thoughts, the expansion of my understanding, and the deepening of my convictions. I've come to understand the profound importance of language and its role in shaping our thoughts, relationships, and the world around us. Language is not just a tool for communication; it is the very essence of our ability to think, understand, and connect with one another. It's a living, ever-evolving entity that demands our attention and mastery. Throughout my academic journey, I've delved into the complexities of semantics, the power of clear and effective communication, and the need for consciousness in using language wisely. I've learned that it's not just about the words we use but how we use them, and the intentions behind our expressions. Language is the bridge that connects us, and it's our responsibility to build that bridge thoughtfully. My decision to attend a Historically Black College or University was not just about furthering my education; it was a choice rooted in a deep desire to be a part of a community that understands the importance of unity and empowerment. It's about reshaping the narrative that has marginalized and oppressed us for far too long. It's about being a voice for those who have been silenced, and offering a hand to those who seek to rise. Success, I've come to realize, is not just about personal achievement but also about being a source of inspiration and guidance for others. It's about creating opportunities, breaking barriers, and making a positive impact on the world. I've discovered that perseverance, self-discipline, and patience are the building blocks of lasting success. As I navigate my path, I've also understood the significance of being present in every moment and seizing every opportunity. Life is a series of pages in a book, and we have the power to write our own story. Each day is a chance to learn, grow, and make a difference. My journey has taught me that success is not a solitary endeavor. It's about building connections, collaborating with like-minded individuals, and lifting each other up. We are all authors of our own stories, and our collective narratives have the power to shape the world. In closing, I want to remind you that every day is an opportunity to manifest your dreams, to discover your purpose, and to share your light with the world. Have faith in yourself, trust the process, and keep moving forward. Life is a journey, and it's the journey itself that defines us. So, write your story with intention, live it with passion, and never stop believing in the incredible potential that lies within you. As I look back on the journey that has brought me to this point, I can't help but feel a deep sense of fulfillment and ambition. The path has been winding, filled with challenges and moments of self-discovery, but it has also been a journey of relentless pursuit of knowledge and growth. Through countless hours of dedication and learning, I've come to understand that true finesse is born from a foundation of expertise. It's not about shortcuts or tricks; it's about putting in the hard work and mastering your craft. It's about studying wisely, understanding the essentials, and embracing the journey, no matter how arduous it may be. My playlists, each with its own story, have become a reflection of my soul and the experiences that have shaped me. They are a testament to the diverse shades of my personality and the cultural richness that defines me. Music has been a constant companion on this journey, a source of inspiration, and a means of expressing my innermost thoughts and emotions. Through connecting with individuals and studying various leadership styles, I've gained a deeper understanding of the qualities that make a leader. Leadership is not a one-size-fits-all concept; it comes in various forms and styles. What sets me apart is my unique perspective, my background, and my commitment to being unapologetically myself. The purpose of life is a driving force that guides my actions and decisions. I've come to realize that my purpose is distinct, just as I am. I am unapologetically me, and I carry myself in a way that may be unconventional but is true to who I am. I believe that embracing our individuality is what makes the world rich and diverse. My time at Morehouse College has exposed me to the teachings of great leaders like Stokely Carmichael, who emphasized the importance of cultural, political, and economic self-determination. The Black Power Movement has left a lasting impact on my perspective, and the call for embracing our blackness and understanding that "Black is Beautiful" has resonated deeply with me. As I navigate the world of entrepreneurship and leadership, I've come to understand the power of belief. Belief in oneself and one's ability to take control of their thoughts and actions is what separates entrepreneurs from employees. Negative influences and external factors may try to deter us, but it's our belief in ourselves that keeps us on the right path. Religion and politics have long been intertwined in America, serving as a source of influence and power. They have played a significant role in shaping the country's history, from the Constitution to justifying acts of violence. Religion, with its core values, influences society's norms, and morality is the compass that guides our actions within that society. In the end, this journey has been a testament to the power of self-discovery, relentless pursuit of knowledge, and a commitment to embracing one's unique path. It's a journey filled with ambition, purpose, and the unwavering belief that we can shape our destinies and make a meaningful impact on the world. So, as I step forward into the next chapter of my life, I do so with the knowledge that the journey has only just begun, and the possibilities are limitless. In the grand scheme of things, as Black people, the pursuit of capital is not our true challenge. It lies in the choices we make on this journey – decisions that extend far beyond the realm of "Black Owned Businesses." To bridge the wealth gap, we must redirect our focus inward, investing not just in enterprises but in ourselves, our friends, and our communities. The process is straightforward: identify the problem, run a diagnostic test, and seek out solutions.

In a world often preoccupied with the true meaning of holidays, this novel advocates a different approach. It encourages us to use these moments to express gratitude for the progress we've made, acknowledging the value of life itself. Amid the hustle and limited time, the narrative emphasizes the importance of relationships. Rather than trying to cut out the middleman, it suggests building connections that lead to mutual profit, recognizing the middleman as the glue that binds everything together. The narrative delves into the significance of goals, not just in writing them down but witnessing their realization. It stresses the importance of healing along the journey, ensuring the enjoyment of the fruits of labor. Recognition may not always come immediately, but the story reminds us that the audience is meant to applaud at the end of the show. Contentment, even in adversity, is a vital lesson. Legacy, deeply tied to beliefs and principles, becomes a focal point. Life's struggles and triumphs, the love shared, tears shed, and the peace found in happiness are all woven into the fabric of peace. The narrative calls for respect, especially towards women, highlighting the role of mothers in our existence. The quest for wealth takes an introspective turn, questioning the value of material riches when the soul holds greater wealth. The narrative, resonant with personal experiences, touches on the power of actions, amplified by the complexion of one's skin. Following directions becomes a metaphor for guidance in real life. As the story navigates through various facets of life, it sheds light on women's struggles, emphasizing the need for continuous reform for their voices to be heard. Political nuances play a role, with an acknowledgment that equal representation is insufficient; descriptive representation, drawing parallels between constituents and representatives, is essential. The narrative weaves through memories, from the laughter of sunny days to the teachings of Grandad and the essence of staying true to oneself. It encourages staying in one's lane, navigating through life's challenges while appreciating the beauty found both in sunshine and rain.

About the Author

Lamarr Futrell is a beacon of inspiration, a catalyst for change, and a visionary leader committed to empowering individuals and communities worldwide. Born and raised in the vibrant city of St. Louis, Missouri, Lamarr's journey is one defined by resilience, compassion, and an unwavering dedication to social justice.

From an early age, Lamarr was deeply influenced by the rich tapestry of his surroundings. Growing up amidst the challenges and triumphs of urban life, he developed a profound understanding of the systemic barriers that often hinder personal growth and collective progress. Determined to be a force for positive change, Lamarr embarked on a journey of self-discovery and service to others.

Fuelled by a desire to uplift marginalized voices and bridge societal divides, Lamarr pursued higher education at Morehouse College, where he immersed himself in the study of sociology and the humanities. It was here that he honed his passion for advocacy, community organizing, and the pursuit of social justice.

Throughout his academic and professional journey, Lamarr has been a tireless advocate for equity, inclusion, and the empowerment of underrepresented communities. He has collaborated with grassroots organizations, educational institutions, and community leaders to develop innovative solutions to pressing social challenges.

Lamarr's commitment to social impact extends beyond the realms of academia and activism. He is also an accomplished writer, speaker, and thought leader, whose insights have inspired countless individuals to embrace their innate potential and strive for excellence.

In addition to his advocacy work, Lamarr is deeply passionate about creative expression and the transformative power of the arts. He believes in the ability of music, literature, and visual media to heal, inspire, and unite people from diverse backgrounds.

As a sought-after mentor, educator, and public speaker, Lamarr continues to make a profound impact on the lives of others, empowering them to find their voice, pursue their passions, and create positive change in the world.

In all his endeavors, Lamarr Futrell remains steadfast in his commitment to nurturing souls, shaping futures, and building a more just, equitable, and compassionate society for generations to come.

www.ingramcontent.com/pod-product-compliance
Lightning Source LLC
Chambersburg PA
CBHW031324130726

47988CB00007B/2970